The Ballad Of Cody Byrne
And Other Stories

RYAN GREGORY FLOYD

THE BALLAD OF CODY BYRNE

ISBN: 0-9985013-6-0
ISBN-13: 978-0-9985013-6-9

DEDICATIONS

To the memories of Jim Harrison and Leonard Cohen. You showed me the way. Here is how I would honor your passings.

ACKNOWLEDGMENTS

Helen Isaacson, Tracie Hebert, and Holly Floyd: you have been my rocks.

Greg Floyd, thank you for being a father to a wayward, but determined son.

To all the many souls who have influenced my life: I'm terrible at directly acknowledging all those who have left a deep impact on me, but here's a start.

My friends: Sam Nelson, Steve Gamache, Diana Searl, Andy Fritzschall, Reid Nicholls, Doug Fettig, Sean Barton, Casey Carman, Adam Engstrom, Catie Quinn, Jennie Merrill, Kelsey Parris.

My paternal grandparents, Bud and Betty Floyd. You are with me often though departed. I always knew I had someone to call when you were still with us.

My maternal grandfathers, Tom Hebert and great-grandpa Isaac, you lonely and wayward souls whose hands passed to me the errancy of desire and the way of the guitar.

My extended and/or symbolic family: John Myers, Tanya Whisenant, Wendy Isaac, Joe and Margaret Epstein, Jep Epstein, Nancy Oswald and Kathy Seligman, David Ensor, Medora and Ken Monigold, Scott and Sophia Davison.

My teachers and coaches: Mrs. Stenkamp, Mr. Deeks, Mrs. Smith, Mr. Bartnick, Mr. Ross, Mr. Hess, Ms. Mckenzie who didn't believe I wrote that story when I was 14, and Mrs. McAdams who did believe it (I wrote that story), Coach Clevenger, Coach Combs, Coach Andresen, Coach Smith, Coach Turnbull, Mr. Kemmer, Ms. Miller, Mrs. McCormick, Kitty Greenberg, Ed Graf, Dr. Cannon, Dr. Manson, Dr. Noble, Dr. Sha, Frank Turaj, and so many, many more.

Lastly, my lovers, whether we were ever made love or just platonically connected. Here's the shortlist of luminous spirits who left a mark on my heart: Courtney, Brittany, Jordana, Caitlin, Roberta, Medora, Erin, Khara, Kelsey, Olivia, Marion, Lynn, Xandra.

CONTENTS

The Ballad Of Cody Byrne

Earthward: A Novella

Short Stories

Song Lyrics

Poems

THE BALLAD OF CODY BYRNE

THE BALLAD OF CODY BYRNE

Άειδε Μούσά μοι φίλη,
μολπής δ' εμής κατάρχου,
αύρη δε σων απ' άλσεων
εμάς φρένας δονείτω.

- Mesomedes, Hymn to the Muses

A TINKLING OF THE CAMEL-BELL

Dolly Mayer lived most of the one hundred and three years of her life in a house on St. Charles Avenue in the Uptown neighborhood of New Orleans. Her father, a wealthy landowner in northern Louisiana, purchased the house for Dolly and her husband upon their marriage. For over a century Dolly had lived the life of a New Orleans aristocrat and philanthropist, eating lunch every week at Galatoire's and maintaining connections with the city's most influential citizens. Shortly after Hurricane Katrina, Dolly passed away in a nursing home near her father's old landholdings in northern Louisiana. She had been moved there after the storm struck, and now her grandson Mo lived in the grand old house on St. Charles Avenue with his wife and stepson, Elaine and Cody.

In one of the bedrooms on the second floor of the house Cody Byrne sat at a desk in the afternoon slant of amber light, the turquoise paint on the walls and high ceilings peeling away, the two bronze statuettes of muses frozen in their respective dancing and violin playing. Despite her wealth and influence Dolly's house had fallen into disrepair over the years, and as he heard the metallic scraping of a streetcar passing out front Cody realized he loved it all the more for its decadence. He felt lucky to be in such a house, in the city of New Orleans, with hours to devote to writing. It was just that the open page of his notebook was blank. It was blank although he'd been at the desk since sunrise. Some days he managed to write a little, some days more, but it never seemed to add up to anything with structure.

13

He wanted to tell stories but he did not know where to even start. At last he picked up his pen, wrote a line and then set the pen back down, staring at what he'd written.

What if I never have a girlfriend?

He'd had flings and he'd had sex, but he'd never had a real girlfriend. He did not seem to be interested in the girls that liked him, and the girls he liked were always unavailable. And so he had managed to get through high school and college without the kinds of experiences that many friends took for granted. When college ended he ran off to live in Italy, secretly imagining that he would meet an Italian woman and live the rest of his life there. He ended up developing a crush on a woman with a boyfriend. When he admitted his feelings to her she was flattered and very kind, and for awhile they maintained a sort of intimate friendship before it became me too painful and Cody had come running back to New Orleans.

The bedroom door opened and Cody's stepfather looked in and said, "it looks like Pompeii in here. Can I talk to you downstairs for a moment?"

Cody followed him out into the hallway and down the winding circular staircase past walls thick with paintings, through several spacious rooms cluttered with furniture, lamps, and more paintings. In contrast, the kitchen was the simplest room in the house, small and just large enough for a little breakfast table. Dolly had never cooked a meal in her life.

They sat down at the table and Cody's stepfather looked out the window silently for a minute, gathering his thoughts slowly as was his habit sometimes before speaking. He was tall, with curly brown hair cut short, a goatee, and large, piercing gray eyes.

"This afternoon when your mother woke up from her nap she said, 'Mo, we need to get a divorce.' And then she started talking about Dolly's money and I just said, 'you need to get a lawyer, because I'm getting one.'"

Cody looked out the window in silence and then asked, "where is she?"

"I don't know. She left after I came downstairs."

"Did she say anything about this before? Why does she want to get a divorce?"

"This is completely out of the blue for me. I have no idea where this is coming from. I mean, you remember the other night when you walked into our bathroom and you heard her laughing in the bedroom, right?"

"Yes."

"We were being intimate."

"I could tell. It was awkward."

"I apologize. I just don't understand what is happening right now."

"Alright, well let's figure out where she is."

Cody pulled out his phone and called his mother.

"Yes, Cody?"

"Mo just told me that you want to get a divorce?"

"This is not something you need to worry about, Cody. Mo and I can handle this. He doesn't need to involve you."

"Why do you want to get a divorce?"

"I can't talk about it right now but listen to me, Cody. Everything is going to be alright."

"Where are you?"

"I am somewhere safe, okay?"

"Mom, can we just talk about this?"

"Right now I need my space and I'm not ready to talk about this with you. You and Mo are too close for me to be able to talk to you about it."

"Where are you, Mom?

"I'm close."

"Don't do this again, Mom, please. You have to tell me what's going on."

"Cody, we will talk about this another time. I will not be home tonight but I am safe and I will call you tomorrow."

She hung up and Cody sat staring at the blinking contact name on his phone.

After several hours of waiting and discussing options Cody and Mo decided to go looking for Elaine. Mo thought she would be in a bar, and so they stopped at several places as Cody walked through

15

looking for his mother, imagining that he would find her with another man, laughing and being intimate. At last he found her sitting alone on the back patio of Madigan's. As Cody approached her table a frown formed on her slender face framed by jet black hair.

"I told you I wanted to be alone."

"Mom, you have to tell me what's going on. This affects me too."

His mother lit a cigarette and Cody looked down at the ashtray that held several butts. He looked to see if all the butts were from her brand of cigarettes. They were.

"Please, just come home."

"I will drive you back to the house but I will not be staying there tonight."

Cody and Elaine drove down St. Charles avenue and parked the car in front of Dolly's house. They sat there in silence for a minute until Elaine's phone chimed at the receipt of a message.

"Who is it, Mom?"

"It's just a friend."

"Mom, let me see your phone."

"No, Cody."

"Are you having an affair?"

"No."

"Then why won't you let me see your phone?"

"What if I was having an affair? What would that mean to you?"

"Don't do this again. You've done it too many times to me."

Elaine sighed and looked out the window. "Cody, I'm not having an affair. And I'm not doing this to hurt you. I have not been happy with Mo for a very long time. I knew the moment I moved here seven years ago that I'd made a mistake."

"But just a few months ago you said everything was great with you guys. Why haven't you said anything until now?"

"I just didn't want you to worry."

"Do you see how destructive this is, though? You keep it all in until suddenly it explodes around you, affecting everyone you love. It happened with Dad, it happened with Olsen, and now it is happening with Mo."

"Cody, I know how much you love Mo, but I can't sacrifice my

16

own needs as a woman just to stay with him. Mo will always be in your life."

"But we finally have a family here, and now you're going to break it up?"

"There is a quote I would like to share with you, 'Do what thy manhood bids thee do, from none but self expect applause; He noblest lives and noblest dies who makes and keeps his self-made laws.'"

"Of course I know that one, it's by one of my childhood heroes, Sir Richard F. Burton. The rest is 'All other Life is living Death, a world where none but Phantoms dwell, A breath, a wind, a sound, a voice, a tinkling of the camel-bell.'"

"Then you understand what I have to do?"

"No, Mom, I don't understand at all."

In December Cody bought a silver scooter and moved into an apartment on Esplanade Avenue a block from the cluster of stores and restaurants that formed the hub of the Faubourg St. John neighborhood in Mid-City. He loved the apartment and the neighborhood the moment he first parked his scooter and looked down Esplanade Avenue at the Greek Revival architecture of the New Orleans Museum of Art in City Park. In front of him stood two stucco houses, a quadro-plex on the left and a smaller two-story duplex on the right tucked back behind a tree. His apartment was on the ground floor of the duplex. It was very small, consisting of a kitchen, a large bedroom, and a short hallway adjoining a bathroom.

Cody immediately bought some white paint and began to paint the kitchen which was a hideous slime green. In the evenings he painted with WWOZ on the radio. Each morning he went for a walk up Grand Route St. John, passing by an old plantation house that faced Bayou St. John, a natural waterway connecting to Lake Pontchartrain. He liked to walk along the bayou trail and sit down on any of the many concrete docks by the water, soaking up the sunshine. He would then start writing in his apartment. One night as he was laying awake in bed he began to see a story like a movie, set in

Ancient Greece. He started writing a screenplay. Cody began to feel, at long last, that he was starting to really live his life.

One afternoon as Cody was cooking lunch in the kitchen he saw a girl getting into her car in the parking lot out back. She was young, and her tired, agitated expression and her messy light brown hair suggested that she had a just woken up from a night out, and now was hurrying to get to class. Cody had not met everyone who lived in the six apartments. Two young women were moving out right as he was moving in, and one of them had offered him some of her furniture. He'd taken a futon.

After lunch Cody got on his scooter and started riding to meet up with Mo for coffee. He drove along the bayou which was sparkling in the bright afternoon light, and turned left on Esplanade to cross the bayou and then left again onto Carrollton Avenue. He was riding between the streetcar tracks in the far left lane. A car in front of him slowed to turn and Cody went to switch lanes. As his front tire crossed the streetcar track and the handlebars grew rigid he knew he was going down. He came down hard with the scooter on the concrete and could hear the brakes of cars screeching behind him. Immediately he sprang up and struggled to lift the heavy scooter back upright. He walked the scooter to the side of the road as someone shouted from a car to see if he was alright. He reached the parking lane, set the scooter on its stand and promptly sat down on the grass by the sidewalk.

His pants and his coat had been worn through by the concrete in several places. He could see the white of bone on his ankle and his elbow. Someone approached and asked if he was alright. He said that he was fine, that he was just a little shaken up. His heart was pounding and his breaths came fast. His body felt numb and distant. Mo arrived after about fifteen minutes followed by his mother, who had happened to be in the city and rushed over when Mo informed her of the accident. She decided to take Cody to the urgent care center in Metairie. They drove down Carrollton Avenue and up Canal Street, and as they drove past the marble mausoleums and tombs of the Canal Cemeteries Cody began to wonder how close he had come to death, and what it would have meant if he had met it.

AMARA

That evening Cody sat in the futon in his apartment, drinking a glass of wine with the lights out and a single candle burning on his desk, as he liked to do in the evenings. He felt like he had almost died that afternoon, and was full of gratitude for the life he still had. His body ached in many places, and yet he sat there feeling restless, wanting to symbolically declare that he was still alive.

He heard a piano melody playing in one of the nearby apartments. It was familiar and haunting, and yet he couldn't quite recognize it. He stood and stepped out onto the front porch to hear it more clearly. There was an immediacy and richness to the sound of the piano that suggested live performance, and yet it sounded so good that it was likely a recording.

He walked down the steps of his patio and along the path that led to Esplanade Avenue. The street was quiet under the shroud of its many live oak trees, and Cody ran his eyes over the shadowy contours of the leaves caught in the streetlights. A soft, cold winter breeze shook the leaves, and the air smelled dry and fresh. How long had it been since he stood on a sidewalk and simply appreciated the light and sound of a street?

The music stopped playing and he heard a door open on the balcony of one of the other apartments, and the sound of a lighter clicking.

"Hey, what are you doing?"

Cody turned and looked up at the balcony. It was the girl he had seen that morning in the parking lot.

"I was listening to the music. I couldn't tell if it was live or a recording. It's beautiful."

"Oh, thank you! I'm just practicing for my juries."

"Juries?"

"Oh, that's just what we call our music exams. We have to perform a piece in front of a jury. Do you play?"

"I play guitar and a little piano."

"That's great! My friend Mike who plays mandolin is coming over soon to play on the balcony with me. Do you want to get your guitar and join us?"

Cody went to his apartment and returned with his guitar and a bottle of wine. He entered her bedroom up a flight of stairs and found her sitting at the piano.

"I'm Amara, by the way. Your name is Cody, right? My friend Anna said she met you when you were moving in."

"Yeah, she gave me her futon."

"Oh, yeah! I used to be roommates with Anna. I could tell you some stories about that futon. Hey, do you want to listen to me play?"

Cody sat down on her bed as Amara began to play Debussy's Arabesque I. While she played he looked around the bedroom. It was densely and colorfully decorated with many photos of friends, ornate masks, and art nouveau posters of exotic locations.

Amara stumbled a little through a section and he saw her face redden. She furrowed her brow and tightly pursed her lips with determination, driving ahead with the song. Cody studied her as she played. Her light ash brown hair was thick and long, flowing down to her shoulders, but her bangs were cleanly cut just above her eyebrows in a way that reminded Cody of the actress Sophie Marceau. She had a small, elegant nose and oval mouth, and her skin was soft and pale with a warm glow. As she arrived at the end of the song she slowly lowered her arms to rest on her lap.

"I love that piece so much. I used to listen it to every day when I lived in Italy," Cody said.

"You lived in Italy? That's so great! My Dad is an English teacher

21

at the Arts Magnet school I went to in Dallas, and every year he takes a group of students on a trip to Italy. It is so much fun. So what were you doing there?"

"Well, I studied there for a semester in college, but after I graduated I went back to teach English in a small city in the Emiglia-Romagna region called Faenza."

"That is so cool. I love Italy. So what do you do now?"

"I'm going to be starting a job with TeachNOLA next week."

"Are you a teacher?"

"No, I'll just be working in the office. I interviewed with the manager and admitted that I really want to be a writer and he suggested that I wouldn't have time to do that if I entered the program. And then he offered me a job in the office. What about you?"

"I'm a senior at Loyola, studying Music Therapy. It's such a nice night. Do you want to go out on the balcony?"

"Sure. I brought some wine over if you'd like some?"

They talked for the next hour drinking wine on the balcony, or rather Amara mostly talked, which was just as well with Cody who rather liked to listen more than be heard. He knew that he could often be too shy, but this night he kept hearing a steady reminder saying, *death almost came for you this afternoon.* What slight hesitation could compare with that hallowed specter? And so when he did speak it was with rare honesty and candor, and whenever Amara's steady stream began to slow the right words always seemed to be there for him, and their conversation flowed swiftly and easily until Mike arrived with his mandolin. For the next hour they played Joni Mitchell and old folk songs on the balcony. Amara had a lovely singing voice, and as they played Cody couldn't take his eyes off her. At one point, Amara stood up and Cody took in her full hips and narrow waist, and the slope of her breasts beneath her tight shirt.

As the wine set in their songs gave way to conversation and laughter, and soon Amara suggested that they should all go to Ms. Mae's for drinks. Cody went to the bathroom and as he walked back through Amara's room to the balcony he overheard Mike saying, "I can tell he really likes you."

"Really? He's so cute. I have such a big crush on him."

The next morning Cody woke up in Amara's bed. The room was bright in the morning light. Amara was asleep with her back to him. As his sleepy mind traced back through his memories of the evening Cody felt an electric thrill course through his body. He was living. He had met a girl and she seemed to like him. He smiled to himself as he remembered reciting Byron's "She Walks In Beauty" to her in the dark bar of Ms. Mae's, her eyes fixated on his, holding her glances a little too long, a little too interested to be platonic.

After a couple hours at the bar they had returned to the apartments together. Amara asked him if he wanted to come watch a video of her favorite comedian, Eddie Izzard, and so they went up to her bedroom and watched a couple sketches sitting on her bed. Cody began to wonder if he should leave soon, if she expected him to leave that night. And then she had asked him, simply and without awkwardness, "hey, do you want to just spend the night?" He remembered taking off his pants and getting into bed with her. There they were, side by side, and Cody did not make a move. After a while Amara turned on her side and Cody put his arm around her, and they fell asleep like that.

Why hadn't he tried to kiss her? He liked her too much. In all of his romantic experiences sex had always been there from the start. He wanted this to be different. He wanted her to feel like he respected her.

Amara began to stir and Cody looked out the window, wondering if it would be awkward waking up with him in her bed.

"Good morning," she said softly.

"Good morning. How are you?"

"Good, hungry. Have you ever been to Koffea for breakfast?"

"No, what is it?"

"It's this great little coffee-shop and restaurant in the Bywater. Let's get breakfast!"

As they drove down Esplanade Avenue in Amara's car Cody felt deep gratitude for the life he was living. Just the day before he had been driving past the cemeteries, thoroughly shaken from the accident, and now he was speeding down Esplanade Avenue under a clear sky on a cool winter day in New Orleans. Amara smiled as she sang along to the radio, and Cody smiled as he looked out at the honey colored trunks of the trees in their bare winter beauty, the light almost golden on the grand old houses of the avenue.

After breakfast they went to Cafe Du Monde for coffee and beignets and then sat on the levee looking out at the Mississippi river. Cody philosophized on the life of the river, talking about the screenplay he had started awhile back about the flatboatmen who used to sail down the river to New Orleans, spend all their earnings in the city that care forgot, and then take the long hike of shame back along the river to their midwestern homes. Amara told him many stories about her family, which was large, close and clearly very important to her. She had grown up with three cousins who were all similar in age. They used to play a game where they were Beatles in the sunlight, and then morphed into velociraptors whenever they entered the shade.

"We still have so much fun together. Last fall I went to stay with my cousins in New York. We were standing on the street and we all looked down into a gutter where there was this plastic ring. We're all looking down silently and my cousin Delilah just starts humming the theme from The Lord of the Rings. Naaa Naaa, naaa na na naa na naaa na."

Cody laughed loudly at this, not just because he loved *The Lord of the Rings*, but because there was something about Amara's story that was so familiar to him. He felt like he understood the humor of it in his bones.

"Would you like to have dinner with me at my house tonight?" he asked.

That afternoon they drove back to the apartments and agreed to meet up again for dinner at seven. In his apartment Cody opened up his notebook and quickly wrote down what had happened the night before. He reflected on it awhile, feeling a warm glow all through his body. The expressions on the faces of the muse statuettes dancing on his desk seemed happier than usual. He began to hear in his head one of the songs from the CD of Ancient Greek music he had been listening to lately. It was called *Hymn to the Muse* by Mesomedes. He wondered what the lyrics meant, so he looked them up online and then slowly translated them with the aid of an Ancient Greek dictionary.

Sing for me, dear muse.
Inspire my melody.
Send a wind from your groves
To stir my restless mind.

Cody sang the song to himself in Ancient Greek. It was beautiful, mysterious and sacred. He stood and paced restlessly around the small bedroom of his apartment, singing the song which slowly morphed into a different melody with different lyrics.
Amara, Amara, I love you like the sea.
He wrote the lyrics down in his journal and checked the time. The little corner store on his block would be closing soon and he needed to get groceries for the dinner he was going to make. He jumped to his feet and left his desk with the notebook still open.

That evening as Cody made dinner in the kitchen Amara walked around the main room of his apartment. It was furnished with a single bed, a dining table for two, and a writing desk. Amara walked over to the desk and read what Cody had written in his journal that afternoon. Silently she closed the notebook and studied the bronze muse statuettes and the Lawrence Alma-Tadema painting of a nude woman reclining. The only other decoration in the room was a copy of Van Gogh's *La Chambre* which hung above the dining table.

In the small hallway that led to the bathroom there was a large bookcase and Amara glanced over the titles. There were a number of classic novels, biographies of various writers and poets, and a whole shelf dedicated to Ancient Greek history.

"Would you like some wine?" she heard Cody calling from the kitchen.

"Wow, it smells amazing in here! What did you make?" she said as she entered the aroma-filled kitchen that was small and painted bright white.

"Rigatoni all'Amatriciana."

Cody poured them each a glass of Argentine malbec.

"Cheers." They raised their glasses and sipped.

"It's good, Cody. You really like wine, don't you?"

"Sure do."

"Why do you like it so much?"

"It always seemed like the drink of poets, like something that would inspire your imagination. And then living in Italy I got in the habit of it. Also, it's better for your health than other drinks."

Cody began ladling the pasta onto two plates.

"So where did you learn to cook?"

"I started cooking for myself in college and got really into it for awhile. Not as much these days but I still cook for myself. I used to watch this show with a guy who would approach strangers in the grocery store and offer to cook them a meal. I learned a lot from that show."

"That's so wonderful! When I was in high school I had a phase like that. I'd watch cooking shows every afternoon after school and then try making all the recipes. I was a little depressed at the time and gained some weight, but at least I learned how to cook!"

Cody set the plates down on the dining table and they sat down to eat. Steam rose from their plates as Cody grated fresh parmesan cheese onto the pasta. The rich bacon-infused tomato sauce merged with the tannic scent of olive oil and the earthy tang of the parmesan. Amara took a bite and followed it with a sip of the wine.

"Oh my god, this is so good."

"I'm glad you like it."

"Thank you for doing this. It's been a really long time since anyone did something like this for me."

"Sure."

"Seriously, it's really sweet of you."

"It's what you do when you really like someone."

Amara smiled and looked nervously around the room. Cody watched her steadily.

"So, I was looking at your books. You have so many!" Amara said.

"I read a lot growing up."

"Tell me about this screenplay you're working on."

"It's set in Ancient Greece and it's based on a true story. Before Athens became a democracy it was ruled by a pair of brothers. One of these brothers fell in love with a young man named Harmodios, whose older lover decided to kill the brothers. He managed to kill one of them. The other became an unbearable tyrant and within a few years Athens overthrew him and became the world's first democracy. I'm still sort of working out the story. The main character is this guy Aristogeiton. And he's either going to be the lover or the mentor for this character Harmodios. I'm not sure how to approach their relationship because I don't think modern audiences can imagine male to male sexuality as the Greeks saw it. There was also a woman involved, a courtesan named Leaena who was also Aristogeiton's lover. After he killed one of the brothers, she refused to say anything when they tortured her, so they cut out her tongue. There was a statue of a lion without a tongue that used to sit on the Acropolis, and they say that it was dedicated to her."

"Wow, that sounds great. You're really into Ancient Greece, aren't you?"

"Yeah. I know that it's a bit ethnocentric, but it's not that I think they were better than any other culture. It's just that they recorded so much about themselves that it's possible to really delve deep into their culture, and in doing so to learn about our culture. There are so many words, ideas and customs that have passed down from their culture to ours that it's hard to not be interested in them."

After dinner Amara sat down in the futon while Cody sat across from her at his desk. He put on the cd of Ancient Greek music and explained to Amara what he'd learned about the music. She listened attentively, and after a while Cody became aware of Amara's green eyes gazing steadily into his own, her hands in her lap and her lips pursed in concentration. He could faintly smell the scent of something like that of lilies, and for once in his life Cody did not mind the smell of perfume.

"I want to kiss you," he said.

"So do I."

He leaned in and softly kissed her lips, awash in lilies as his mouth moved down kissing the length of her smooth, pale neck, breathing in the warm softness of her hair. He felt like he would be happy to stay like that forever.

They kissed some more and then Amara prepared to leave to go to a party for two of her friends that were moving away. She invited Cody but he politely declined. He was starting his new job the following day and would be staying at Dolly's house that week while his scooter was being repaired. After kissing for a few minutes in the parking lot Cody watched Amara pull away in her car. He stood there looking in the direction of the driveway for a long time, feeling as if his heart was in the sky.

DOLLY'S HOUSE

The next morning Mo drove Cody to the office of his new job, a single room of cubicles in a larger complex across from the levee of the Mississippi, minutes from Dolly's house. The manager was a tall, dark-haired man in his mid-thirties, and would be leaving the office later that year to pursue a PHD in history. He introduced Cody to his coworkers, two women in their late twenties who had started out as public school teachers, and then set him up in his cubicle with a laptop. For four hours Cody replied to emails about the program and recorded data in a heavy-handed management app. Gradually he grew accustomed to the various expressions and acronyms that were casually thrown about the office: "Charter," "Magnet," "selective admissions," "open enrollment," "POC," "RSD," etc.

During his lunch break he walked to the levee and looked out at the river as he ate an open-faced sandwich of whole grain bread topped with thick slices of feta cheese and carved chicken breast. As the tanker ships passed slowly along the river Cody tried to concentrate on his screenplay. He had decided that he would write every day after work, and he hoped to use his free moments at the office to plan scenes. It was difficult to think about anything steadily after all the coffee he had drunk that morning to focus on the work. He smoked his first cigarette of the day, appreciating the bright light of dopamine reward that warmed his mind after such a long abstention. He had been chewing nicotine gum all morning but it had hardly allayed the cravings.

In the afternoon Cody worked for a few more hours before walking back up Broadway Avenue toward St. Charles. As he walked he hummed a melody to the lyrics of Yeats's "The Lake Isle of Innisfree." When he arrived at Dolly's house he sat down at Mo's grand piano in the living room and began working out the melody he had been singing.

After about twenty minutes of playing Mo walked through the front door of the house. Cody heard him walk into the kitchen and a short while later he returned with a drink in hand.

"I drove by Rose's house and there was a man helping your mother move."

Cody rose from the piano.

"Who was it?"

"I'd never seen him before. Younger than me."

"I'm sure he was just a friend."

"Why haven't I ever heard of him, then? I've been married to her for seven years and she never tells me about the attractive male friend who's now helping her move? I'm sorry, how are you? How was work?"

"It was good. A little slow. Do you want to talk?"

They walked into the room that Mo had set up as his studio space.

"I just feel like such a fool," Mo said, slumping back into a sofa chair.

Cody saw the misery in his face and wished he could help. For seven years Mo had been like a father to him, but more than that he had become Cody's closest friend, and a mentor to boot. Mo composed and recorded music for commercials and documentaries. He self-deprecatingly described himself as a "jingle-writer" because he hadn't broken through as a famous musician years before. But in Cody's eyes he was an artist. His mastery of the piano and his ear for music inspired Cody. He'd bought Cody his first guitar and had always encouraged him in his writing and his artistic aspirations.

"Don't be so hard on yourself. We have no idea what's going on with Mom right now."

"I feel like I have a pretty good idea what's going on with her."

"Well, I hope that's not true. And until we know what's true there's no sense torturing yourself."

"I suppose so. You seem to be feeling better, by the way. The new place is working out?"

"Yeah. And I met this girl that lives in the apartment next to me. She's a musician."

"Ah, a girl. And what is the fair maiden's name?"

"Amara."

Mo fairly exploded with delight, standing up and singing, "Amara, Amara, I'll love ya, tomarrah."

Cody laughed as Mo walked around the room singing.

"So I see what's going on," Mo said. "Amaaaaraaaa. At least one of us is getting something out of this mess."

"I didn't say that."

"I can tell though. You have a glimmer in your eye that tells me so. You like this girl."

"Maybe…."

"You can't fool me. Let's go get some dinner at Basil Leaf. There's a beautiful waitress that works there. Maybe your good luck will rub off on me. 'Amara, Amara, I'll love ya, tomarrah.'"

After dinner Cody went upstairs to his old bedroom and sat down in the sofa chair. Amara had told him that she was going to The Columns Hotel that night to see John Rankin play. Cody felt like he should stay in and try to write. He had a melody for a song, and an image of walking along Bayou St. John with her. In the past, he would have stuck it out even if he didn't write anything. Tonight felt different though. There was a restless energy in him, an urge to see Amara. He stood up and walked down the hall to Dolly's old bedroom, which had become an entertainment room. Mo sat reclining and nursing his customary Jameson's and water, watching a tv show.

"Do you feel like going to The Columns to meet up with Amara? John Rankin is playing."

"Might as well. I'm not getting any younger here."

When they arrived at The Columns Hotel Amara was sitting at a table with some fellow students. Her face beamed when she saw

Cody walking up. She jumped up and hugged him. John was on set break and so Cody, Mo, and Amara walked into an adjoining room to sit with their drinks. Mo proceeded to fill in Amara on what was happening with Elaine. She listened attentively as he laid out the full story, finally responding diplomatically,

"It does sound strange that she never told you about him. But it's probably not a good idea to jump to conclusions, especially with everything so fresh."

"Well, kids, I should probably head home," Mo said. "It's getting past my bedtime."

"I can take you home later, Cody," Amara offered.

After parting ways with Mo, Cody and Amara went to Ms. Mae's where they stayed until nearly sunrise, playing songs on the jukebox and smoking cigarettes. That night Amara stayed at Cody's apartment and drove him to work after they had slept about an hour. He felt a little delirious as he struggled through only his second day at his new job. He couldn't wait to see Amara again. During a smoke break he looked up at the sky and could feel a warmth and excitement coursing through his body like he'd never felt before.

Amara picked him up after work and they went back to Dolly's house for dinner. Mo was out for the evening and they had the grand old house all to themselves. Cody made pasta again for dinner, fettucine alfredo with the recipe from the original restaurant in Rome. After dinner they took their wine upstairs to Dolly's old pink room where they began making out on the bed. Amara said that she was ready, and he asked if she was sure. She nodded.

As they took off each other's clothes Cody felt suddenly awkward and self-conscious. He hadn't even had sex with anyone in over two years and he felt rusty. At first she was under him, and then she moved to straddle him. He was in awe of her like that, the way her body moved in the lamplight of the room, the ceiling fan spinning above her. The dull screeching of the streetcar passing down St. Charles Avenue rumbled through the old house. He could feel himself right on the edge of it, and he wanted to make it last but all at once he realized he had lost control. He tried to stop Amara's hips from moving but it was too late. He could see the disappointment on her face after. She lay down beside him and said,

"Maybe I should head home."

"No, stay."

The rest of the week flew by and they made love nearly every chance they could, in the morning upon waking, after Amara picked him up and they got back to the apartments, and at night after dinner. At the end of the week they went to the first parade of Mardi Gras, Krewe Du Vieux. They danced and made out in the streets, and snuck away into little corners to do more. Cody had never experienced such intense sexual desire for someone in all his life. It seemed to grow and expand as his feelings for her developed.

One day during his lunch break Amara picked up Cody from work and they drove along The Fly, the southern stretch of Audubon Park that faced the Mississippi. It was raining heavily and they parked near the Tree Of Life, a huge live oak tree near the walls of the zoo. The rain came down in heavy sheets as Amara straddled him in the passenger seat. Cody pulled off her shirt and bra, kissing her smooth, perfect breasts. She rotated around and lifted her skirt, undoing his zipper. He admired the curves of her shoulder blades as he entered her. She leaned back into him and he smelled the lily scent of her skin, his hands reaching around her breasts and down to stroke her clit. They came together with the rain beating against the windows of the car.

"I love you," he said as his head fell back against the car seat.

That evening after work Cody walked over to Dolly's house because Amara had a late class. When he arrived all the lights were off in the house, although Mo's car was parked out front. In Mo's studio he turned on a light and noticed several bottles of Jameson's carelessly spread about. He walked slowly up the stairs of the dark house, breathing its old and stale air. He walked into Dolly's room and turned on a light, but the room was empty. Perhaps Mo had gone out with someone and they had picked him up? He walked down the hallway to his old bedroom and opened the door. Even before he turned on the light it struck him all at once as he saw the shadow that hung in the center of the room. He ran to the body and lifted it, shouting for help. He grabbed the fallen chair that lay on its side and used it to untie the knot around the ceiling fan. Mo's body fell to the floor and Cody placed a hand on the cold neck to feel for a pulse. In the bluish light of the room from the street lamps outside he could just barely read the words scrawled onto a piece of paper hanging from a necklace around Mo's neck: *Elaine did this.*

SANTORINI

TWO AND A HALF YEARS LATER

Cody woke from a late siesta on a cot in a hot little tent. The blue lighting the walls of the tent told him that it was shortly after sunset. Someone in the campground was playing tentatively on a bouzouki, probably one they had purchased in the village that day, and he could hear little half-wrought melodies and chords on the clear-ringing metallic strings. Despair filled Cody and he reached for his water-bottle of wine mixed with water. He took a long sip and felt it burning its way to his stomach. On the other side of the tent Amara slept peacefully, her long hair stretched across the pillow and her angelic child's face in repose. For the thousandth time Cody felt a little surge of love as he looked at her. But love was always mingled now with flashes of anger at this little woman whose life had become so entwined with his own. She would be going to Morocco soon, and after that who knew what would become of them? Slowly it all continued to unravel. Love was like some beautiful building made perfect in a day, followed by years of watching it slowly crumble. Last night had been such a night. Another pillar had come crashing down.

They had been sitting in a bar perched on the cliff of Fira overlooking the caldera bay where the island's volcano had stood long ago. She was sipping a tropical drink and admitting that she was attracted to other people, even to the busty blond waitress who brought them their drinks. He told her that he was also attracted to other people and always had been. So went another little lie that they had told each other to sustain the perfect illusion of love. It was in such moments of brutal honesty with each other that her heart opened and she clutched at him again. Her eyes were moist and pleading. She hurt and yet she felt love for him in the potent way of their first months together. Kiss me, she said, and yet he waited. He was drawn to her sweetness and her lush body but repelled by the honesty of it all and the return to solitude that again awaited him. They talked more and she admitted to wanting to date other people. She had said it before but now it was with absolute certainty. Cody was too captured by the truth in that moment to hurt or to express any emotion, and it helped her to continue her confession. She said that she'd blamed him and criticized him so many times when it was really that she wasn't ready. She wanted to feel free and unrestrained, not because of a desire to sleep with other people, but simply because for so long their closeness had made it impossible for her to do as she wanted, to have experiences without the constant compulsion to worry about another's feelings. For so long she had hated herself for wanting to have more experiences in spite of having the "perfect" man.

Cody's thoughts drifted now to Crete a week before. She had worn her bright yellow dress and black cap with her hair running out the back in a thick amber mane. Her skin was tanned and shone with a clear delicate youthfulness that was irresistible. As they hiked through the canyon from Matala they passed a series of ancient graves and caves hollowed out of the cliffs. Goats wandered through the dry fields and clambered up the rocks to sit on the steepest precipices.

After a long descent down a rocky trail they reached Red Beach, infamous for its popularity with nudists. A lone shack stood at the head of the beach selling beer, coffee and rented umbrellas. It was a thin sand beach surrounded by rough hewn cliffs like massive velvet cords, and they turned down the beach away from the cluster of umbrellas. They passed a lot of people still dressed but the majority were bare to the skin, including a family that had chosen an overhang in the cliff to make their shelter. They set down their stuff and stripped off their clothes. Her lovely body was bare to the world and Cody felt his lust rising. They rushed down into the water which was warm and felt amazing on his skin. She came close and he held her body to him but she squirmed away laughing. Cody rolled in the waves beneath the hot sun and felt the water caress and invigorate his body. Stepping out of the waves and walking back to the towels he was very much aware of being naked in front of a beach full of people. He sat down and took note that they appeared to be the youngest nudists on the beach. And then he watched as she emerged from the water like some goddess or nymph, her wet skin shining and her flesh lush and delicious. He felt his dick tingling with pleasure and an almost painful, adolescent lust. She sat on the towel next to him and he had to turn over on his stomach as she reclined with beads of seawater rolling down the contours of her body.

A naked little girl walking along the beach stopped right in front of them, squatted down, and peed into the shallow waves.

PAROS

After lunch they went upstairs to their bedroom to rest for a few hours before going back to work. It was warm in the room and they lay on the bed in their underwear. The ceiling fan spun lazily above them. Cody was trying to read a book he'd grabbed off Claudio's bookcase, but he was distracted by Amara's body beside him. Getting in bed after working in the sun for hours tended to make him horny.

"Can I masturbate to you?" He asked her. She nodded, continuing with her reading.

He started masturbating looking at her flat stomach leading up to her full breasts in her bra, the skin smooth and pale. He imagined them on a beach, the two of them naked in the sun after swimming. He leaned over and smelled her hair that lightly rested on the elegant curve of her shoulder. She set the book down and watched, her hand running slowly down the length of his torso and rubbing his thigh. His hand reached down to stroke her pussy through her panties. They kissed and then with his teeth he pulled aside her bra strap so he could lick her nipple. Amara's head rolled back.

"I want you inside me."

He pulled down her panties and rolled on top of her. As he was about to enter she said, "this still means we are going to break up, ok?"

He paused for a moment.

"Ok?" she asked.

He murmured in agreement and put his dick inside her. It didn't matter anyway. Nothing mattered in that moment but to be inside her and to feel her underneath him, her hips moving as he drew closer and closer to coming. He wanted to spend the rest of his life like that, fucking her and about to come inside her. When he did come though and had rolled off of her he thought about how strange sex was. Such a constant and inescapable energy, and when it was over you wondered at what had obsessed you so. Yet the absence of desire seemed almost a fiercer torment than desire itself, the malaise of satiety after the excitement of hunger.

Amara had come not long after he'd entered her. It had always been easy for her, and in the early months together they had always come together.

That evening Cody sat at the desk in their bedroom and looked back through the moleskine journal he carried on their travels. Amara was downstairs in the living room watching a British comedy, and he welcomed the time alone to think. He went slowly through each entry, searching for some thread to connect all of the experiences. The only thread he could find was the lingering desire to have a room to himself where he could create music. New Orleans would be a good place for that, he felt, but he could not imagine leaving Amara. He came to the end of the entries, and flipped forward to the end of the journal. There was a card tucked into the back pocket. He removed it: an anniversary card. Amara had painted a beach scene with him standing like Zorba on the sands. On the back she'd written a note:

I cannot believe that we have known each other for only two years! It seems as if you have been a part of my life for much more. I want you to know how much you mean to me. You are my best friend. I love remembering all the wonderful times we have shared, from crazy Mardi Gras nights to just sitting on our porch with Stumps and Willy as our entertainment.

These are just a few things that I love about you...

Your impeccable intelligence. The way you never belittle me when I ask questions that you've known years before. And you always have the answer!

Your gorgeous face! You are the most handsome man I've ever known (or seen!).

Your love of life. Knowing that you want to make a mark on the world shows your strength and determination.

Your love for music! I am able to rant with you about certain songs or even phrases in pieces. Your expression of emotions the music gives you.

The fact that I can tell you anything and you understand and accept me for who I am.

I love you Cody Byrne and I am so grateful to have you in my life.

Thank you for always being there, holding my hand down this path, and especially for being there to hold my hand when we let go sometimes. You are my sexy man! I love you, Rienzo! Happy Anniversary. - Amara Byrne.

When had she given it to him? Only six months ago, in Italy. Could things have really been that much better then, or was it just one of those lulling moments in the middle of a storm? He tucked the card back into the journal pocket and started a new entry.

How did it happen? It resides in my mind like a dream you desire to never leave. Love is a great and unexpected gift in life. From others' reports we know it will be amazing. We desire it and seek it, but obstacles always emerge and it never quite works out. Slowly we learn to lose hope and plod on doing what we love, until suddenly one day it is happening. Love is there and it is exactly as always imagined, as always desired. Every day we marvel at the joy of it, and every day it grows stronger and more pervasive, until one day, completely unexpectedly, the first shadow falls on the sunlit Eden. A small argument, the possibility of diverging interests or information from the past revealed — whatever it is it drives the first knife into love's bliss. Months and years may follow still together, yet after the first shadow there can only be more rainy days ahead, and from then, although the love always lives in memory and in flesh, it is a constant effort to keep the shadows from overtaking the light. Such is love. Its perfection is short-lived, yet so perfect we can hardly ever regret all that follows, no matter how bitter and scornful.

He remembered one day when they lived together in the little shotgun apartment in New Orleans. Amara had gone for a walk to the neighborhood coffee-shop, and when she returned she read him what she'd written in her journal. It was about how Cody reminded her of the character Jules in the film *Jules et Jim*, which they had recently watched. She wrote that sometimes she imagined Cody

40

would be like her Dad had been with her Mom, that she could just go out and mess around with anybody and Cody would always be there, waiting for her. He had been furious with Amara when she read that aloud. Why hadn't he seen it even then? And why was he so angry when she was telling him her truth? What kind of a fool was he to stay with her? It always came down to that decision he had made: he couldn't walk away from love, not like his parents had.

His life before Amara seemed like somebody else's life, and not one he wanted to live.

CORFU

I looked up from my notebook and out across the dry yellow fields of barley in the late morning sun, the sounds of crickets a steady hum. It was another hot day on the Greek island of Corfu, and the heat had a way of settling in the main valley of the island where I sat on the balcony of our hotel. The writing had been going well, so well that I'd forgotten where I was. It was enough writing for one day. I reached for my pouch of drum tobacco and papers, and rolled a cigarette. I sat there smoking and drinking my strong cup of instant coffee, staring down at my brown legs in my white shorts with the folded cuffs. There were a few stains on the shorts from my coffee, the last pair I had that weren't completely unwearable and sitting in a pile under the bed. We would have to do some laundry soon in the noisy washer at the end of the hallway. I thought about the clothes spinning in the wash and then hanging in the sun on the back patio on the portable laundry line we carried with us in our travels.

I began to wonder what Dorian was doing. Maybe he would be ready to eat lunch soon. He always loved to cook food and eat, although I wondered if he wasn't growing tired of eating in so much. Before long he would get fed up with the routine and demand a special meal, and I would agree to it because otherwise he'd start an argument about money.

I finished smoking my cigarette, stubbing it out in the plastic ashtray and looking out again at the fields that ran to the green rolling hills along the periphery of the island. Corfu was supposed to be a magical island, the setting of Shakespeare's *The Tempest*, and the setting of Odysseus's stay with the Phaecians whose hospitality and abundance were renowned. What of it all now though? The island was an island, greener than the Greek islands of the Cyclades that ran like a spine from the Greek peninsula down towards Crete. It was green because it sat in the humid waters of the Adriatic, a crossway between Italy and Greece, but still an island like the rest. Was I growing disenchanted with this land I had longed to see for so many years? Dorian on the other hand seemed delighted by the people and the life of the island. Every interaction with locals seemed to convince him further of the greatness of the Greeks.

I decided I would go find him, and so I gathered up my notebook, my Lawrence Durrell book and my coffee and walked down the hallways of the abandoned hotel. There was something reassuring about having an entire hotel to yourself. The owners were doing extensive renovations and so kept it closed for the summer, but were happy to get a little money from a couple of backpackers who didn't mind not being waited on.

Dorian was not in our hotel room. I found him out by the pool, lounging in a chair with a book in his lap. He was talking to one of the Albanian workers the owners had hired to work on the hotel, a young man who looked to be in his early twenties. I had seen him before. He liked to work with his shirt off and had attractive broad shoulders. As I approached I heard him say, "yes, I will have to show you some time, my friend," before turning and passing me with a respectful greeting.

Dorian looked up and said cheerfully, "hey, what's going on?"

"I'm getting hungry. Do you want to make some lunch?"

Back in our room I cut up some cucumbers into slices, diced some tomatoes and slivered some red onions, mixing them in a large bowl with olive oil, crumbled feta cheese and dried oregano. Dorian warmed up some of the tomato and eggplant stew we'd had for dinner the night before. As I made the salad I tried not to think too much about the Albanian guy. I wanted to ask what they were talking about, and why he'd said that he'd have to show Dorian, but I knew it would infuriate him. As we sat down at the patio table to eat Dorian asked, "how did the writing go?"

"It was good. I started a new story."

"That's great, what is it about?"

"I don't want to talk about it yet. It's still fresh."

"Okay," Dorian said, looking a little annoyed and taking a large bite of the soup. "So how about we go to the beach after lunch?"

Every day it was the same. Dorian didn't seem to be capable of standing a day without some time at the beach.

"Yeah, maybe. It might be good to keep working though this afternoon."

"Well, I could just go by myself and you could stay here and work?"

I wished now that I'd said differently. "Are you sure you want to go to the beach? I mean, we've gone every day this week."

"Yeah, I'll just go by myself and you can work."

"It's okay, I can go with you."

"I think I'll just go by myself."

I looked into his green eyes which had narrowed on mine. "Are you sure? What if I want to go to the beach?"

"It's clear that you don't because you didn't say you wanted to go at first."

"Maybe I needed time to think about it."

"I think I need to just go by myself."

"Why?"

"So I don't feel so dependent on you all the time. We've talked about this before. You have to let me go a little."

"Did you just want to go by yourself all along? Why did you even ask me then? Why didn't you just say you were going to the beach by yourself? Maybe I want to go too so we can pick up some snorkeling masks."

"Alright fine, but I want to be able to go to places by myself sometimes. You have to let me do that."

"Of course. I just feel like going today."

After lunch we took the scooter down the bumpy dirt road that cut across the valley, passing through yellow fields and a golf course that looked in need of watering. We turned on the paved road that carried us from the flatland of the valley to the beach road that ran steeply down past rolling green hills thick with tall Italian Cypress trees, down to the narrow, rocky beach of Ermones. There were only about fifteen people on the beach that afternoon, and Dorian and I decided to try taking the thin trail that skirted the edge of a mountain and disappeared around a jutting cliff.

The hike did not last long, the trail ending above another small, secluded harbor like the beach at Ermones. The emerald water looked welcoming below us but the way down was steep and rocky. We decided to backtrack to a place we'd seen with easier access from a grouping of massive, sea-smoothed boulders.

"We can go skinny dipping," I said. "I don't think anyone will see us."

The water lapped against the boulders that were warm in the sun as we removed our swimsuits and donned the snorkels we'd bought on the way. With a loud shout Dorian jumped into the water and I followed after him. Instantly I was plunged into a bright, brilliant blue world full of fish. For awhile I swam alone along a reef that went deeper and deeper until I could not see the bottom beyond the reef. The water felt colder too and with a shiver I imagined a shark behind me and quickly made a few circles in the water, looking into the depths.

I swam back toward the boulders and found Dorian clutching the bottom of a boulder with his hands and peering under it. Then he launched off the boulder and like an arrow shot along the reef before making a lazy turn and slow ascent to the surface. As we made our way back toward the boulders I admired Dorian's body through the water. It was even more stimulating than usual. The strength of his muscular legs as they kicked him forward was clearly on display.

We climbed onto the boulder and lay in the sun. I felt a little dizzy from the cold water and Dorian's body. I looked over at him. His eyes were shut, beaded drops of seawater falling from his hair onto his face and down his chin, down his chest and the grooves of his stomach. I reached out and ran my hand along his thigh toward his penis. He looked as if he was going to say something and for a moment I imagined it would be his usual, "that's not proper nudist conduct." I leaned over and took his flaccid penis in my mouth, and heard Dorian sigh a little. He hardened and filled my mouth and my hand reached down to stroke my clitoris. I felt so close to climaxing and just wanted to feel his penis inside me. Dorian's head arched back and he made a sudden jerk and said that someone was coming. We both sat upright with our backs to the trail as a middle-aged couple passed us silently. I could feel the blood pounding through my crotch and my head was dizzy and floating far from me. The couple disappeared around a bed and Dorian began putting on his shorts.

I wanted to keep going because the couple would not return for a little, but I knew Dorian was already over it. We decided to go back to the beach and see what the menus were like at the restaurants at the end of the beach. When we reached the beach someone waved to us from the sand and we saw that it was Pietro, the husband of the woman who owned the scooter shop. He was an Italian who'd been coming to Corfu for years and had fallen in love and married Daphne, an Athenian who spent the summer months on the island. As we approached Pietro smiled widely, his teeth very white against his uniformly tanned skin. We sat down beside him and I talked to him awhile in Italian as Dorian walked down to the water and went swimming.

Pietro and Daphne were beautiful people who lived in the sun and the sea. They both had long dark hair and perfect bodies. Pietro had always been very kind, and had invited us to come see him at the bar where he worked in the evenings. As we talked I absent-mindedly looked down the length of his body to the tiny green thong he wore that did not hide anything. Pietro smiled and caught my gaze again. It was curious, this feeling that he might have an interest in me, and yet he seemed happily married to such a beautiful woman and they were clearly perfect for each other. I felt a little caught off guard and looked out away at the sea where Dorian was coming out of the water. I told Pietro that we were going to see about getting some food at one of the restaurants and he said he hoped we would come see him at the bar one evening.

I wasn't really hungry but Dorian wanted to try the moussaka on the menu of one of the restaurants, and so we took up a table that looked over the sea. Dorian ordered a beer and I asked for a red wine and then decided to order an omelette. It felt good to be under the shade with the wind coming off the sea. Dorian looked happy, his long hair streaking back as his green eyes shined. "So what do you want do tonight?" he asked.

"Um, I'm not sure. What do you feel like doing?"

I thought about my writing and how I would have liked to stay in and work on it but I could sense that Dorian wanted to do something else.

"Why don't we go see Pietro at the restaurant and then go down to Agios Gordios?"

"Yeah, that could be fun."

Dorian looked out at the water. "Why don't you ever get excited about doing stuff?"

"I do get excited. I'm just trying for us to save money and work on creative stuff like we planned, that's all. I'm not against doing stuff. Going out sounds fun."

"I can't wait to move into Robin's house in the village. It will be so much easier to go do stuff. And that piano, ooooh, I'm so excited."

"Tomorrow's the day."

"And then my Mom's coming in a week and will take us out to dinner every night and show us all over the island."

I dreaded the arrival of his mother. It would mean the end of my long sessions writing alone. I said nothing about it though, taking a deep sip of the Greek red wine that ran straight to my empty stomach with a flutter.

We did not go out that night. After eating lunch the owners of the restaurant insisted that we drink a bottle of the wine from their family vineyard. They were very friendly and curious about us, wondering how it was that we were just wandering around Europe indefinitely. We did our best to explain the service industry jobs we'd had in Dallas while living with Dorian's parents, how we'd saved up for months and had been able to travel for so many months by working on organic farms through the WWOOF program, and doing other similar work-away programs. These seven weeks on Corfu were going to be our vacation, the one time we did not have to work on farms. It was also to be our creative time, for me to write and for Dorian to work on music.

We arrived back at the hotel drowsy from the wine and the meal and both of us got into bed and were soon asleep. I woke up to find Dorian sitting up reading from the Kindle, and it looked as if the sun had just set. I leaned over and wrapped an arm around Dorian's waist. My thoughts drifted back over the day we'd spent and the moment on the boulder before the couple interrupted us. My hand reached under the sheet and up Dorian's leg but he shifted a little and said, "don't." I rolled away and lay there stewing in it before getting up and walking into the bathroom to shower.

The warm water poured over me as I sat in the shower. Showers had always been a calming place for me, a sort of primordial womb where I was safe. I was horny and I hated that I was horny, hated that Dorian never wanted to have sex anymore. It hurt me so much and just made me want it more. My hand reached down and began to massage. I began to imagine Dorian and I on the boulder again, but then saw a woman there instead, a woman with blond hair and big breasts. I imagined them meeting on the trail and striking up a conversation, agreeing to explore the trail together. I imagined them deciding to go swimming, and Dorian simply dropping his shorts wordlessly in front of her and diving into the water, leaving her struck by his nonchalance and following suit. They snorkeled together and shyly admired each other's bodies under the water. Later, sitting on the boulder Dorian looked over her wet body glistening in the sunlight. The woman noticed him getting hard and let him touch her. I came hard and quietly in the shower and I knew Dorian had no idea.

Dorian was not in the room when I got out of the shower. After drying off and putting on a pair of still slightly damp but clean shorts I went up the stairs of the hotel and followed the sound of a tv to a room where Dorian lay on the bed watching an American film with Greek subtitles. He was silent as I entered and I knew that he was sullen.

"Did you still want to go out in Agios Gordios tonight?" I asked.
"It's too late."

"Are you sure? I know you were really excited to go."

"Let's just stay in. We should have gone straight to Agios Gordios from the beach instead of coming to the hotel."

I'd wanted to come back to the hotel after the meal, knowing that a nap would clear my head. Dorian had been irritated but relented. He knew I could be difficult when I hadn't slept enough.

"It's not too late. Come on, let's go out."

"No, it's too late and I don't want to anymore."

I pleaded with him a little more and gave up, heading downstairs to write. I was sure he felt misunderstood and unappreciated. Back in the room I gathered up my notebook, and a bottle of Greek red wine and walked out on the back patio. The night was warm and thick with moths that circled the patio light. I sat down at the table and looked out across the fields where music was coming from the gypsy camp. There was a nearly full moon in the sky. A bat swooped overhead. Greece was such a strange place. One moment it was a magical paradise and the next thing you knew it was a moonlit night with music from a gypsy camp and bats overhead.

I read through my story and felt less excited about it. The writing was so simple, like a fairy tale, although I knew the story wasn't. There was a lot I didn't know yet about the characters though. I could start to see them, see her sitting on the plane with a headache and drifting off to sleep, him waking up in the almost empty bedroom that he also used as a studio, the mattresses leaned up in the corners for soundproofing during the day.

When I finally got into bed Dorian was sound asleep already. I could feel the wine really kicking in, a torrent of emotions straining my ability to keep track of any single thought. I felt so much anger at Dorian. It had been this way with him for such a long time, months and even years at this point. Why couldn't things get better with us? Why couldn't he desire me as I desired him? Why did I put up with all of his shit? The answer was simple. Two and half years before on a January day we had met and quickly fallen in love and those first four or five months had been the most beautiful experience in my whole life. Everything leading up to it seemed a pale shadow of a life in comparison. And it was in the intensity of that time that my feelings for him had been tempered out of such durable material. I knew that I could never leave him, because leaving him would mean letting go of the most beautiful moments of my life.

The next morning it took three trips on the scooter to carry all of our stuff from the hotel to our new house in the village of Sinarades. It was a quaint village, and our house sat at the end of a cobblestone alley and had a large raised garden and patio out back. After settling our stuff in the bedroom Dorian sat down at the piano and began slowly playing a score that had been left there. I walked out on the balcony and looked out over the terracotta rooftops and the hills. Here was where I would write every morning.

That afternoon we drove the scooter down the winding road that led to the seaside town of Agios Gordios, a densely packed series of restaurants, bars and cafes whose largest building was the gaudy Pink Palace hostel. The beach was much larger here than Ermones, and the water was quite shallow.

CASANOVA

NINE MONTHS LATER

It was a warm spring night when Cody parked his scooter on the sidewalk next to the Circle Bar. Tonight, after six months apart, he was going to see Amara again. As he walked into the intimate bar he remembered one night a couple years back when he'd come there with Amara after having dinner with Mo at Dolly's house. They'd shared a bottle of wine at one of the candlelit tables in the corner, talking invariably about how much they loved each other. On the drive back to his apartment Amara had gone down on him. He remembered the challenge of keeping his eyes on the road while she did that.

The bar was about half full as the band played away tucked into the pentagonal corner area with windows that looked out on Lee Circle. On Sunday nights the band grilled food out on the patio. For many months, Cody had made a habit of coming there every Sunday, and he'd made friends with the band members and the other people who liked to come on Sundays. It was a pleasant thing to do each week, and many times he'd thought about how much Amara would have liked it.

Lauren walked into the bar and they went outside to sit on the stoop.

"I don't know if I should tell you, but Amara's coming tonight,"

51

she said.

"I know. Rachel told me."

In the months since returning from Europe Lauren had been his closest, albeit most inconsistent, friend. At first he had wondered if something romantic would happen between them. Perhaps he'd even hoped for it, imagining them in a naked embrace in the shower or in the rain, something appropriately sexual and poetic. On her birthday they'd stayed up late at Mimi's and when he'd gone in for a kiss she'd turned away. She'd been drunk, saying that she thought he'd always be in her life and that they were soul twins. After the failed attempt at a kiss he'd gone to the bathroom and came back apologizing. He felt like a typical male, no different than the hordes of men that made their pilgrimages to Bourbon street strip-clubs to stare at naked asses. She forgave him. He drove her home on his scooter that night, and she ran into the house shouting back, "I love you." She confused him.

They went back into the Circle Bar to get fresh drinks. Cody recognized a couple of Amara's friends walking in, and he walked over and hugged several of them. And then she was there, all five feet and six inches of Amara beaming at him.

"Hey," she said, and the high pitch of her voice struck his ears pleasantly. They hugged.

"You look so good, Cody."

"So do you."

They talked briefly. She had driven in from Texas just that day. Morocco had been amazing. Somebody came up to talk to her and soon they were separated. Cody went back to the bar so he could listen to the band, but glanced back over at her once in awhile. She was busily chatting with her girlfriends, and her face was animated and excited. She seemed happy. It was so strange to see her there in person again.

The band started playing a song he'd come to love and he listened intently to its slow verses building into a chorus that had several girls standing up and dancing in the small space. One of the girls was obviously a dancer and her slender arms moved in slow, graceful arcs. He felt a tugging on his sleeve and looked down. It was Amara.

"Well, it was so good to see you. I think we're going to head on. I'm so happy that you're doing well."

He could think of nothing but to lean forward and kiss her. The lips were soft as he remembered. She looked at him with concern in her eyes when he pulled away.

"Cody, don't do that."

All at once her girlfriends swooped in saying things like, "we should get going. It was great seeing you, Cody." And like that she was gone, and the band played on in front of him while Cody stood at the bar. He turned and walked into the restroom. There was a single stall without a door, but Cody walked into it and stood above the urinal as if to pee while he cried. Awhile later, after he had done his best to wipe away the evidence of his tears, he walked out quickly through the bar and out to his scooter. He wondered where Amara had gone next, but knew that it didn't matter anyway. She didn't want to see him.

He drove through the CBD and along the outer edge of the Quarter, passing through the Marigny and over the railroad tracks on St. Claude. The gaudy neon sign of the Saturn Bar drew him in. It was dark inside, and a band was playing in the balconied room that adjoined the bar.

Cody walked over to the bar to order a beer. To his right there stood a girl wearing a skin-tight dress cut short across the thighs. She was sucking on a lollipop and staring at him. They started talking. She told him about her son who was named after Oliver Stone. He asked her if she wanted to go sit on the balcony and listen to the band. They went up the stairs and when he sat down she seated herself on his lap. The singer of the band growled out words to a swampy back-beat. He breathed the coconut scent of her hair and felt the curves of her hips in his lap. Her head turned and they kissed. He could taste the strawberry flavor of her lollipop.

"You looked so sad when you walked in."

"I'm not sad anymore."

She kissed him some more and he wondered once again what exactly a woman could find attractive in a heartbroken man. Once he'd started going out again he'd been surprised to discover that women were not bothered by the intensity of his interest in Amara. He talked openly about her to anybody who would listen, confessing that he was still in love with her and that he hoped to win her back. Perhaps women just took him for what he was, and were relieved that he did not expect anything more of them than the pleasure of their company. Perhaps they were content to enjoy the company of a man infused with the heightened sensitivity of heartbreak and still hard-wired to connect deeply with the opposite sex.

Later that night Cody drove his scooter down North Robertson along the overpass while she followed him in her car. He turned up Esplanade remembering the many nights at Amara's side driving back to their neighborhood of Faubourg St. John. The bayou was dark and he saw the wakes of a few nutria swimming away from the shore as he passed.

They pulled up to the apartment on Dumaine St. that Cody had just moved into. It was a large duplex and he shared one side of it with two other housemates. They went up the stairs and entered his room where there was a bed, a fold-out office desk, and a bookshelf without the shelves installed. He closed the door and pulled her to him.

"Do you have any music?" she asked.

"No, I just moved in."

She messed around with her phone for a moment and set it down next to the bed. Hip-hop music played from the phone while his finger-tips grasped the bottom of her dress and slowly pulled it up over her body. He kissed her breasts and they fell back onto the bed.

"Do you like them? I just had them put in."

His hands felt the wetness of her vagina as he kissed her tasting the sugary fruit and vodka of her energy drink cocktail.

"You can come in my mouth if you want."

Cody wondered at her experiences. Later, after he came he held her and reflected on how much he wished he was holding Amara. She left very early in the morning, waking him from a deep sleep with a kiss. He barely caught her words and fell back to sleep with the blurry image of her walking out the door of his bedroom wearing her tight dress with a tiny white purse swinging along her hips.

SARA

TWO YEARS LATER

They lived together in a small creole cottage on north Rampart street in the Bywater. The house was painted blue with red trim and had a large front courtyard where a bougainvillea always in bloom poured over the roof onto the colored tiles of the patio. Sara was a dancer and taught classes to public school children. Cody worked construction and taught guitar to twenty-somethings hoping to broaden their horizons. For awhile they were very happy together.

One day they took the ferry out to Ship Island off the Mississippi coast for the afternoon. As he stood with Sara on the bow of the boat he could feel again that sense of boundless adventure like he remembered feeling when he was nineteen. As the seawater sprayed intermittently across the bow he could feel a secret thrill thrumming in his gut and coursing down his legs and up into his chest. He felt like good things were ahead, and he wondered how things could have gotten as bad as they had gotten at times in the past. Maybe now was the turning point. How often though had he felt this before, only to be plunged again into a dark stretch? There was no telling what was ahead, but there was always hope, and in this moment the hope in Cody was like a fine fire illuminating much of the scenery around him.

Sara leaned back into him and he wrapped his arms around hers, caressing the smooth skin of her wrists, lightly sweeping down over the knuckles of her hands. He pulled her closer to him and breathed in the scent of her hair. He kissed her neck and looked back out at the waves rolling by.

"Look, dolphins!" he said. Other people on the bow began pointing at the arching fins of a pod in the distance. He remembered Zorba's words of criticism, "what kind of a man doesn't like dolphins?" He wasn't that kind of man. He loved dolphins, and he loved the sea and sun, the wind off the bow and Sara in his arms.

They arrived in front of the old circular stone fort of the island, disembarking down a long pier and in the shallow green water Cody could see small fish darting among the fronds and algae. They passed up over the grassy dunes and proceeded down a wooden bridge that led through the treeless marshlands of the island's interior.

The white sand beach lay on the far side of the narrow island. There they swam in the warm water as the waves carried them up and down. She said that it was their first time in the sea together and that it was special. He knew the sea was sacred to her. She had grown up right near a sound on the east coast, and she still spent the holidays at her family's home in Barbados.

After spending a couple hours reading and sunning on the beach they decided to walk down the length of the island to try and see East Ship Island. There had once been a single Ship Island, but a hurricane in the middle of the last century had separated them into distinct islands, one accessible by ferry and the other only by private boat. They hoped to go camping one day on East Ship Island. As they walked down the beach together he found himself wondering at how beautiful it was to walk the wet sands under a blue sky with the woman he had come to love so much. He pulled her aside and kissed her and they walked on arm in arm.

After about twenty minutes they could see the end of the island in the distance. The grassy marshes at the center of the island gave way to rippled tidal sands as the island narrowed at its tip. It was here that they saw the turtle. It faced the water and stood but ten feet from the lapping waves, and yet as they approached it did not move and at last they reached it and saw that it was dead, its head and arms decaying in the sun. Suddenly the once refreshing smell of saltwater and wet sand became instantly a scent of decay. They agreed that it seemed like an omen and that they would not continue to the end of the island. They turned around and started back down the long stretch of barren sand.

Once more he found himself reflecting on his happiness. It seemed like something he had once known and could dimly remember. Something was so familiar about this moment, about being in love with this woman in a perfect place. He pulled her aside again to kiss, and she said that she wished they could have sex on the beach. He continued kissing her and his hands moved down her body, his kisses moving down her neck and breasts. He looked down the beach again and went to his knees, pulling down her bottoms and letting his tongue settle in the sweet warm groove of her vagina. As he did it he could see himself from a distance, on his knees going down on this woman, his hands tightly clenching her ass and pulling her hips into his head, her hands clasping his head and her head thrust back in the air.

He was hardly aware of how long he was there doing it, but after quite some time and after they had fallen to making love in the sand he saw a jet-skier approaching. Quickly she pulled her swimsuit back on and he pulled up his shorts. The jet-skier did a few spray-filled turns and then headed back away from them. He wished he hadn't told her someone was coming. They realized that it was getting late and that the ferry was probably loading up already for the return trip, and so they continued down to the beach where all the day umbrellas had been folded up, across the island over the marshes and down the wooden planking past the fort. The ferry was ready to depart and the ferry workers yelled at the two of them to hurry up or they would get left behind.

Despite their shouts he paused for a moment to read an informational sign about the lighthouses of Ship Island. Apparently there had been several over the centuries, destroyed by fire or storm and then rebuilt. The sign also told of the keepers. One of them had been married with children and his family had lived with him in the guesthouse. He heard the shouting again and so he turned towards the ferry, looking back once more at the sign as he walked. Something about it had grabbed him and made him look at it. Even now with the ferry men shouting and the passengers anxious to start back he felt some compulsion to keep reading the sign.

As the ferry pulled away from the island he remembered that the name of the wife of one of the keepers had been the same as that of the woman who now stood leaning into him scanning the sea for dolphins. He wondered if that had been his reason for reading the sign so intently. A wife by the same name. Could it be a sign for him, of what she meant to him and could mean for him one day?

That night back in the cottage he gave her a long massage with oil that led into sex. As they made love he told her how much he had wanted her all day, how sexy she had been coming out of the waves in her thin bikini, how desirable she was to every man alive. He told her she was the perfect woman for him, that he wanted nobody else. As he came he imagined for a moment that this woman could be the mother of his children.

That night as she slept beside him he began to wonder about their day at the beach, about the turtle that was trying to return to sea, about his feeling of happiness, about having sex with her on the sand and yet being interrupted, about the sign and the keeper's wife. What could it all mean? He looked at her profile sleeping in the dark room and smiled to himself. He was a fortunate man.

Two months later she left to go to a Dance Festival in Maine where she would be interning for several weeks, followed by a trip to Canada for a week with her parents. The night before she left they went to a wine bar that had a large outdoor courtyard and live music. Earlier at the cottage they had finished a bottle of wine together over dinner, and now as they were finishing another bottle at the wine bar they were feeling very warm and friendly to each other. This was a marked change from previous weeks during which they had fought bitterly about many things.

She had been upset when he had missed her dance show on account of his own music show that night. He was hurt by her criticism of his construction job, of her insistence that he needed to be pushed to make changes in his life because nobody else pushed him. Their arguments had steadily worsened until she asked him to move out of the cottage shortly before leaving for Maine.

Now though as they sat outside in the warm July night drinking wine and leaning into each other everything seemed well and good between them. Her month-long absence would be difficult for them, they agreed, but they would get through it and come out stronger for it. Early the next morning as they drove to the airport she complained of a headache and he complained of how early it was, which upset her because it seemed ungenerous. Still, as they said goodbye in the drop-off area of the airport she began to cry and said she'd miss him so much. He said it would pass quickly and they would see each other soon. He watched her from the car as she walked through the doors and down the hallway of the airport until she was gone.

He took a long drink of the coffee in his water bottle and slowly pulled away from the curb. Back at his apartment in Mid City he crawled into bed and slept deeply for several hours before waking to go work at the shop.

LAUREN

TWO YEARS LATER

In the evenings he would lie upright in bed, drinking watered wine and watching shows on Netflix. In his moments of silence in the dark bedroom he felt like the wine was an organic infusion that connected him to the world. To borrow from a popular tv series, he felt like Bran connected to the wisdom of the weirwoods. His mind would travel through his experiences, and he would reach out for the ones he had loved: Amara, Sara, Lauren. Where were they now? He wondered if they could feel him in some way, over the distances that separated them? Perhaps a passing thought of him, no more. Cody didn't believe in psychic abilities, but perhaps he wanted to believe in the idea that he could still communicate with those he had loved. Was he just lonely? What was this desire to be close to people who had long since ceased to care about him anymore?

The density of experience, of memory, of consciousness. It all washed over him, washed through him. He remembered that night with Lauren and her sister when they went to the river with a guitar. It happened that summer just before Hurricane Isaac, before he'd fallen in love with Sara. They sat on the charred remains of a burnt-out pier, playing songs and drinking wine. Before them stretched the Mississippi, the far bank like a string of Christmas lights from the oil refineries. Every once in awhile a large tanker passed, its spotlights searching the river. A storm was moving in and it began to rain, hot drops of water falling through the air. They left the pier and hid the guitar from the rain in a bunch of bushes. They were drunk now and decided to go swimming. Cody took off his clothes and waded into the warm water breathing the faint scents of oil, mud, and rain. He felt the muddy bottom under his feet and waded out to a sandbar where he sat drinking from a bottle of wine. In the distance a wall of clouds rippled with streaks of lightning, the thunder a dull booming carrying over the water. Cody grabbed a handful of mud from the bottom and held it in his hands. He wondered about his Cajun grandfather, about the people who had come to this land generations before. Was this place in his blood somehow? His ancestral homeland?

The girls undressed and joined him in the river. He reached for Lauren at one point hoping to embrace her but she deftly swam away. Lauren's sister joined him on the sandbar and they kissed. She smiled at him as if they now had some secret between them. Lauren got out of the water and started walking up the bank away from them. They shouted at her and she came back down to the water while they sat on the sandbar.

Many months later, after the fallout with Sara, Cody and Lauren had met up on a spring evening to drink wine by the river again. This time they did not go swimming, but wandered into the Quarter where they drank at a bar in Pirate's Alley. Cody admitted to having feelings for her. Her immediate response had been, "I'm not going to have sex with you." He wondered at how she had jumped so quickly to that conclusion. She brought up that night they'd gone swimming in the river.

"It was too much like a male fantasy come true," she said.

"But you said that I'd been good to her, that I'd showed her a gentle kind of love."

"I don't believe that you have feelings for me. The next time I see you you'll have some beautiful girlfriend and you'll deny ever saying you loved me. What happened to Sara anyway?"

He never did tell her about Sara that night. Perhaps it was too painful to admit that within a week of his release from the Psychiatric Ward

61

Sara was falling in love with someone else. What struck him as harshest was that he had nursed Sara through her frequent illnesses, but when his turn had come to be sick she had abandoned him for someone else. They had met up a few times after that day on Bayou St. John, but she had always hidden the truth. He'd learned about her moving on months later from a mutual friend. The news was devastating to him. Before that, he had hoped that their paths would realign in the future. He'd spent many nights awake thinking of her, missing her, hoping she wouldn't move on. When he learned the truth it broke the last thread that still held him to love, like a guitar string tuned up until it snapped. After that he resolved to not let anyone in again. With that resolution he had directed all of his energy into music and writing.

AMBULANCE TO LAFAYETTE

Cody lay awake in his bed with the lights out. I've got to cut back, he told himself, as he took a sip of wine mixed with water. If he did so gradually he knew he could get back to a better place with it. He just needed time, and peace. He could set aside his projects for awhile, let the album wait. This was more important at the moment. The darkness of the room amplified the intensity of his thoughts. What was happening to him?

A few days before his mother had woken him from a nearly comatose drunken nap. He remembered her hand on his arm, and her words, "Cody, I'm worried about you." The next thing he remembered he was standing at the bottom of the stairs shouting up at her, "you don't understand me. I'm a poet." He was clawing at his chest for dramatic effect. And all at once he'd woken up, as if from a dream, standing there at the bottom of the stairs, the slam of the kitchen door resounding in his ears. He went up the stairs and found his mother and her husband standing in the kitchen. He saw the fear in her eyes. He apologized profusely.

Now Cody walked out the side door of the house and along the front to the mailbox. It was a hot July afternoon, and there was no mail. He looked down the street and saw two police cruisers moving slowly down the street. He wondered what was happening on the block and paused to watch them. A few houses down there was a house that regularly attracted the attention of the police. The cruisers parked in front of his house. Two officers stepped out and one

63

addressed him,

"Are you Cody Byrne?"

"Yes."

"You're not in any trouble here. We're not arresting you or anything. We have what's called a coroner's warrant instructing us to take you to East Jefferson General Hospital for a medical evaluation. Think of it as a fancy taxi ride."

Cody struggled to piece together the officer's words. They wanted to take him to the hospital? It struck him that these were probably his stepfather's friends. Maybe his mother just wanted to scare some sense into him.

"Do you mind if I get some shoes on in the house?"

"Not at all, but we'll have to escort you. Sir, I have to ask this, are you armed?"

"No."

The officers followed him along the side of the house, through the side-door and into his apartment. It was dark and difficult to see anything after the brightness outside. Cody turned on a few lights and walked toward the back of his studio to get his shoes.

"So you're a musician? This is a pretty sweet setup you've got here. What do you play?"

"Thanks," Cody said, slipping on his black leather shoes. "I play guitar and sing."

The officers looked around the studio, impressed by the gear and instruments as they followed him back outside.

They opened the back door of the first cruiser. The officer handcuffed him and helped him into the back seat.

"So, could you explain a little more why you're taking me into custody?"

"We have a coroner's warrant stating that the patient has intent to harm himself or others and requires medical evaluation."

"That's not true at all."

He saw his mother approaching the vehicle.

"What is going on?" he asked her.

"Everything is going to be alright, Cody."

"Mom, don't do this. Please don't do this."

"There's no other choice."

"Mom, please, you know what this is like for me. Please, there's another way."

"This is the only way, Cody."

The cruiser began to pull away and Cody looked back at his mother standing in front of the house. He was in shock. What if it wasn't all a ruse? It couldn't be any more than that, though. They couldn't just walk up and take you to the hospital against your will, right? The officer turned on the radio.

"So, what kind of music do you play?"

Cody thought for a moment about the absurdity of having a conversation about music with the officer who had just handcuffed him. At least he had a little wine in him, he thought.

"Folk, singer-songwriter stuff mostly."

"That's cool, man. I play guitar a little, mostly rock."

The officer went on to tell him about his friends who were in a band, and about his favorite show, *The Walking Dead*. Cody had started watching the show lately, and wondered about the effect of its unmitigated violence on his psyche. *Breaking Bad* had been his show of choice in the days leading up to his visit to the psychiatric ward. The officer chimed in,

"Thanks by the way for making it so easy on us, picking you up, you know."

"So where are you taking me to at the hospital?" Cody asked.

"We'll take you to the ER where we'll hand you over to the hospital staff."

Cody imagined them walking into the ER and his mother and stepfather standing there, the police taking off the handcuffs and saying, "well, it looks like you're clear to leave this time." He imagined driving back to the house having learned his lesson. The officer was quite friendly, after all. He had to be a friend of his stepfather's. A flicker of doubt ran through his mind and he struggled to hold back his discomfort. He knew from experience that a visit to the ER could cost thousands of dollars. He didn't even have medical insurance.

His mother and stepfather were not waiting for him when they arrived at the emergency room. The police handed him over to a heavy orderly who escorted him to a small room with a window that looked out into the busy brainstem of the ER. He was instructed to keep the door shut. After a while a nurse entered and read the content of the coroner's warrant: "patient is exhibiting manic rages, racing thoughts, suicidal intentions."

"What? None of this is true. I'm not suicidal at all. I had an argument the other night with my mother. First she woke me from a nap and I yelled at her. Later that night she said I had to stop drinking, and I said I didn't want to stop, not at that moment at least."

"Unfortunately, when claims like these are made we have no choice but to treat them as truth."

"This is insane. You can just say somebody is suicidal and send them off against their will to a hospital?"

"Yes. You could say the same thing about her and she would be right here instead of you."

"Can I call her or something?"

The nurse made arrangements for him to make a phone call. Cody had to dial four or five numbers before remembering the right one. Cell phones made it easy to forget even the most important phone numbers. His mother answered,

"Hello?"

"Mom, I'm sorry. They're holding me here and I don't know yet where they're taking me. Can you please just tell them that I'm not suicidal?"

He heard her say, "he's crying" away from the phone.

"Cody, we didn't feel safe in the house with you."

"I'll leave then. I won't stay at the house."

"What, and go back to that commune living?" He hadn't quite heard her and asked her to repeat. "Commune living" came back with full force, and in the midst of everything Cody had to suppress a laugh.

After much haranguing his mother agreed to come in and tell

them that the claims were not true. It didn't matter however. The nurse visited him again, clearly upset by the interaction with his mother.

"Well, your mother was very rude to me. Unfortunately, once claims like these are made it doesn't matter if she retracts them."

Cody spent the night in the small room of the ER. He managed to fall asleep for brief periods as the alcohol slowly left his system. In the morning he was told that they would be driving him to a clinic in Lafayette. He rode 128 miles strapped into a gurney in the back of an ambulance with a nurse who sympathized with his situation. The man looked over his file.

"Hmm. Nothing in your system but alcohol, not even marijuana. A musician who doesn't smoke weed. You're a unicorn. Hey, maybe if you smoked a little more and drank a little less you might be in better shape."

Cody deferred to his medical expertise in the matter. They arrived at the clinic in Lafayette where he was taken into an office and went over his story for the tenth time. The nurse was friendly and remarked that perhaps he'd write a song about the experience.

After his interview they led him to the common room where all the patients were eating lunch. About twenty-five people sat at the long white tables in the room, some wearing their own clothes and others wearing the blue scrubs and yellow sock booties like Cody wore. He found a seat at a table in the corner, nodding at the five other men sitting around it. They seemed friendly enough. Lunches were distributed individually, the nurse calling each patient by name. Spaghetti and meatballs was the dish of the day. It came with a salad, some white bread, and milk or juice. At the table the patients traded different items. Cody pushed his juice to the middle of the table and offered the white bread to the man nearest him, who took it readily. In return he ended up with a couple extra salads and a milk.

A man entered the room and introduced himself as 'The Chief.'

As the man began lecturing them Cody looked around the room and took stock of the patients. The five females in the group were all seated at one table near the front of the room. The patients at most of the other tables appeared either severely depressed or were sleeping with heads down on the tables. Apparently Cody had instinctively gone to the table with the liveliest group.

The Chief went around the room asking each patient to introduce themselves. One patient answered with a wandering rant, and one of the patients at Cody's table whispered that he'd overdosed on synthetic marijuana. Another fresh arrival introduced himself. The Chief asked why he was there and he responded, "vacation."

Cody's turn came and he introduced himself. The chief asked him why he was there.

"Drinking."

Appreciative murmurs.

"And what is your goal for today?"

"To get the hell out of here." There was a round of laughter among the patients. Cody continued, "I don't even understand why I'm here. I'm not depressed at all. I wasn't seeking help for anything. I had an argument with my Mom. She said I had to stop drinking and I said I didn't want to. Next thing I know two cruisers pull up with a coroner's warrant and escort me to the hospital. I didn't even know you could do that."

Some of the patients murmured sympathetically. Chief started in on a story.

"Anyone here like collard greens? When I was a kid I hated collard greens. But you know what, my Mama used to pile them up on my plate and she'd say, 'you're not leaving the table 'til you finish those greens.'" And you know what, now I love collard greens. I eat them every chance I get. You know what your Mama did, Cody? She sat you down at the table and she said, 'you're gonna eat your greens, son.'" The Chief broke into wild laughter and was joined by the rest of the patients. Cody couldn't help laughing as well. The Chief grew more somber,

"I wouldn't get your hopes up too much about leaving today. They don't like to release people with the weekend coming. It's too agitating. Now I hope things are gonna work out for you here. We're here to help you, but you're gonna have to put in the effort too."

68

Cody soon grew accustomed to the routine of the clinic, which revolved primarily around meals and the smoke breaks that followed them. He learned that the clinic was one of the last remaining in Louisiana to allow smoking. It was a significant upshot. Cody had never understood the idea of attempting to treat people with psychiatric problems while plunging them into the frantic discomfort of acute nicotine withdrawal. He made friends with a guy named Mike, who was twenty-five years old and grew up in the same town Cody's grandfather had lived. Mike was friendly with one of the girls in the clinic, a fiery girl prone to agitated outbursts during which she would start pacing the common room shouting that "somebody better get me some goddamn medicine for my bipolar." Mike and the girl would often stand in the corner leaning into each other.

At night Cody struggled to fall asleep, reliving in his mind the day two cruisers pulled up to his house and took him to the emergency room. It had been such a pleasant July day, perfect for sipping iced red wine in the shade of the covered patio. Perhaps there was material for a song there. When he finally managed to sleep he often woke a few hours later in a cold sweat. The clinic was kept very cold, and he'd wake up shivering, pulling the thin sheets tightly around him. Dawn came eventually, and Cody would watch the blue light gradually growing from the small window of the room he shared with a schizophrenic patient who spent most of the day sleeping.

While getting his morning medication one of the nurses looked at his hands and commented, "you've got the shakes." Cody looked down at the fingers trembling slightly. The nurse continued, "you went to college?"

"Yes."

"You could become a teacher?"

"I already know what I want to do."

"But you could be poor the rest of your life."

"There's no shame in being a starving artist," Cody said indignantly, quoting an interview he'd read recently with the author of *Mad Men*, one of his favorite shows. The nurse sighed and went on to the next patient. Cody wondered if the author of *Mad Men* had ever been in a place like the clinic.

On his third day in the clinic Cody met with a doctor for the first time. The meeting was brief, with Cody retelling his story and emphasizing his desire to be released as soon as possible. The doctor was frank, taking off his glasses and looking across the desk, "I don't think you're suicidal, but we're not going to be able to release you before the weekend. Look, you went to college, right? You understand the concept of legal liability? If we let you go now and anything were to happen to you it would be a liability for us."

Cody resigned himself to a weekend in the clinic, when the staff was pared down to just a few nurses. Instead of meetings and goal-setting sessions, the patients were set free for long hours in the recreation room. They played foosball, table tennis, and cards while various movies played on the television. Cody was able to get one of the nurses to open up the piano. He banged out "House Of The Rising Sun" despite his limited piano chops. His fingers felt rusty and dis-used, charged with nervous tension.

Aside from the brief moments of distraction, time passed slowly in the clinic. After inquiring into Cody's sleep, one of the nurses learned that his roommate was a snorer, and made arrangements for Mike to become his new roommate. As they settled into their beds that night Mike tossed Cody a paperback novel.

"I like that book, man. It's about vampires. I'd never read a book all the way through, but that book really got me."

Cody thanked him and read a few pages before turning out the bedside lamp. He'd seen the movie and the rainy environs of the Pacific Northwest in the story weren't doing much for him.

"Cody?"

"Yeah?"

"What you gonna do when you get out of here?"

"Get back to making music. What about you?"

"After this? I'm going to a halfway house in Baton Rouge. They've got a job lined up for me there. You have any kids?"

"No. You?"

"Yeah, I got a couple. You didn't ever want kids?"

"Not really. There was one time I got a girl a pregnant, but we decided to get an abortion. I felt pretty bad about it, but neither of us were really ready for it."

Mike mulled this over. "Hey, how many brothers and sisters you got?"

"One sister. What about you?"

"Nine of us total. And they're all messed up."

"Holy shit, that's a lot of kids."

"Yeah, my Mom and Dad didn't mess around. I don't know, man, I feel like the only thing that makes me feel any better is when I'm with a female. There's so much anxiety in me, so much pain, and then a girl touches me and whoosh, it's gone."

"I know that feeling. There was this girl I fell in love with a long time ago, for the first time. When it ended with us I was all broken up about it, and the only thing that made it feel any better was chasing women."

The conversation trailed off and Cody tried to sleep. He could hear Mike tossing and turning in the bed next to his. Eventually he heard Mike get up. For a moment the bright lights of the hallway outside illuminated the room and then it was dark again. Cody fell asleep thinking about the camaraderie he felt toward Mike, and about how the situation in the clinic had a way of bridging the emotional divisions between people of diverse backgrounds. For perhaps the hundredth time since entering the clinic Cody felt that he didn't really belong there. His problems were mere shadows of the mountains the other patients faced.

The following morning Cody entered the common room for breakfast. The room was in a commotion with one of the female patients standing and shouting across the table at Allison.

"Fuck you, you little slut. You're not going to take my baby away from me. I'm here and I'm doing what I got to do to see my little baby and then you bring in that fucking guy in the middle of the night. No fucking way."

Allison walked out of the common room and down the hall, slamming her fists against the windows between the common room and the hall. Cody walked over to the corner table where Mike was sitting with his head down on his arms. Allison stormed back in and shouted at the room as a whole before walking out again. "Y'all know

71

what this is about, this is about a white woman and a black man and y'all are just racists."

One of the nurses announced that they were going to take a smoke break and everyone gathered near the door that opened up to the courtyard. They walked out into the early morning heat and spread out across the courtyard. There was a palpable tension among the patients. Cody and Mike walked along the perimeter of the basketball court.

"So what happened?" Cody asked.

"Last night I went to visit Allison in her room, and her roommate woke up with us in the bed and started shouting. I don't know what's going to happen."

"They can't blame you for trying, right? Nobody ever told me you couldn't do that."

"You're my boy, Cody." Mike hugged him.

Visiting hours were held that afternoon, and the patients without visitors were confined to the recreation room. Cody sat at a table drawing abstract designs next to a girl who'd arrived that day. She admitted to him that she was only there because she didn't have money to pay for treatment of the injury to her knee, so her mother had claimed she was suicidal.

"I talked to Allison on the phone," Mike said. The staff had chosen to release her that day. "She's already drinking, partying."

"Damn," Cody said. They laughed. "Did your Mom come?"

"Yeah, she did. My brother came too and he was blazing like a motherfucker. His eyes were all wide-open, bloodshot and shit."

"Was it good to see them?"

"Yeah, but I've been thinking. You know how people are always saying, 'everything's going to be alright'? They say that because they want you to feel better, but I keep wondering, what if it's not going to be alright?"

One day Cody spoke to his Mom over the phone, and she announced that he had a month to move out.

On Cody's last day in the clinic one of the nurses brought her guitar and Cody played on it briefly before exiting the common room making a peace sign with his hand.

Cody had fantasized that he would walk out the door of the clinic and there would be a girlfriend waiting for him in a convertible with a glass of iced red wine and cigarettes. They would drive away from that place and never look back. Instead Mike and Cody walked out of the clinic where a taxi waited to take them to the bus station.

SPROUT

NINE MONTHS LATER

Cody Byrne, exquisitely sensitive scion of potato farmers, man of the world, child of the universe, fell off the bed after orgasming on the bare ass of a twenty-three year old in his dingy apartment in New Orleans.

"Don't fall off the bed!" she said as he dragged his naked body back onto the sheets and reached for the towel still moist from earlier exertions. They laughed together as he mopped up the scattered remnants of his genetic future from the curves of her bare cheeks. Hygiene completed, he lay back with his head on the pillow and watched the ceiling fan spinning away. His legs felt shaky and a warmth like that following a swim in cold water spread through his chest. As often happened to him after sex, he felt suddenly awkward, as if he should say something but knew that it would come out all wrong. With the seed went all the bluster and confidence of desire. But he felt good, and he reached an arm under her neck and pulled her beside him. She reached down and played with his still semi-erect but softening cock.

"I want to come again," she said. "It's gonna be awhile until you're hard again, isn't it?"

He looked down at his manhood in her small, tattooed hand and wondered at the fragility of masculine desire.

"Tell me a story," she said.

"Once upon a time there was a girl who ran to the forest. She went there because she felt like nobody understood her, not her family or the few friends she had. But in the forest, among the trees and the tall grasses, she did not feel so alone. There were birds that sang to her, and squirrels that chased each other around. One day as she was sitting on a dry, gray log in the middle of a clearing, she suddenly felt like she was being watched. She looked around but there was no movement aside from the quarreling of some blue jays darting from limb to limb and squawking at each other for obscure reasons. She felt the same way the next few afternoons, and one day as she squinted into a particularly dense array of trees and bushes, she caught a slight movement. All at once she grabbed her walking stick and ran at the bushes. There was a rush of movement that became a brown-haired boy running away from her. She burst through the bushes shouting, "hey asshole!" and hurled her walking stick at him like a spear. The sturdy piece of oak hit him on the back of the thigh and sent him tumbling to the ground in a mushrooming cloud of dust.

He looked up to see her standing over him, walking stick in hand.

"What the fuck, asshole?," she said.

"I'm sorry."

"What are you doing, you fucking creep, just staring at me?"

The boy looked around desperately for a weapon, or some words, but neither were to be had.

"If I ever see you again I will fucking kill you." She rapped the walking stick against a nearby stump for emphasis, turned and disappeared through the trees.

She did not see the boy again. A few weeks passed, and the forest began to seem once again adequately boy-less for her tastes. But one afternoon as she came to her favorite log she discovered a piece of paper nailed to it, with a single sentence written in a strained attempt at cursive:

And I looked and I looked at her, and knew as surely as I am to die that I loved her more than anything I had seen in this world, or had hoped for in another. - Lolita, Nabokov

Her first impulse was to tear it up, but something stopped her. She unfurled the lower half of the paper and looked at where the boy had drawn the four parts of a dog's paw."

The girl interrupted his story to ask, "did that really happen to you? Did you do that when you were a kid?"

"Haha, no. Something like it though…" He paused for a moment in thought, and then jumped up and began pouring a glass of wine from the box of Franzia Cabernet that sat on top of his bedroom refrigerator. He poured her a glass and returned to the comfort of his bed.

"What is better than wine in bed," he asked, "and a daylong fuckfest?"

"If you tell me the rest of the story maybe I'll let you come inside me."

Cody took a long and appreciative sip of the wine. He felt like smoking a cigarette.

"Oh, well eventually they end up starting an intensely sexual relationship that ends with pregnancy, abortion, and suicide. Just your run of the mill Garden of Eden sort of thing."

"You love that garden thing, don't you? It kind've turns me on."

"Just you and me thousands of years ago, a naked man and a naked woman running into each other in the middle of the wilderness. We'd be like miracles to each other. We'd fuck and fuck and there would be babies and we'd just do it."

"So you want to put a baby in me?" she asked, laughing.

"Yes. Beautiful musical babies."

"You're crazy."

"For you."

"I think I'm just going to end up hurting you."

Cody took another long sip of his wine. "Well, I can enjoy it while it lasts, right?"

She reached down and started fondling his cock, which stiffened at her touch. She leaned her head down, threw back her hair and began to lick and suck his cock. His fingers massaged the dimple above her ass, his eyes settling on the curve of her waist. He could smell the animal scent of her pussy. With another toss of her hair she looked up at him and laughed while holding his wet cock in her hand. He'd come to love the way she smiled, how her normally brooding face utterly transformed, the laugh that accompanied it unrestrained, light, full of sunshine.

"Sooo, do you want to come inside me?"

The next morning Cody woke with a start, reached out an arm, and patted the bare sheets next to him. "Where was she?" He struggled to piece together the events of the preceding night. He'd played two shows that night, the first at a hole-in-the-wall bar on Frenchmen. The small place had been packed with people waiting to eat at the restaurant above. An eager tourist had insisted on buying multiple shots of Jameson's for the band. While almost strictly a wino, Cody had given into the man's enthusiasm and generosity, with predictable results. He remembered the slice of the band's pizza that had fallen on the ground in between shows which he'd scooped up and devoured. He stifled a gag. But what had happened with the girl? He vaguely remembered getting out of her car and fumbling with his keys in a door which turned out to be the door to the house next to his.

He opened the metal water bottle on the bedside table and poured some wine mixed with water down his parched throat, reached for his phone and called her.

"Hey," she said.

"Hey, how's it going?" he asked with his best attempt at enthusiasm.

A prolonged silence, and then, "I'm good. How are you?"

"No more whiskey for me."

"Oh, yeah?"

"I just can't handle that shit anymore. Why didn't you spend the night? I woke up and reached for you and you were gone."

"Do you remember telling your bandmate that I'd been playing with your dick in the car?"

He pawed at the cobwebs of his memories. Yes, he had done that. "Oh, goddamn it. I'm sorry."

"You should be. You're such an asshole sometimes. Do you remember falling asleep at the bar? I just didn't want to deal with it anymore so I dropped you off at your house, and good thing I waited a moment because you tried to go into the wrong house."

The weight of his misdeeds pressed upon him. Striving for some sort of British aplomb he replied, "so I was thinking maybe we could get coffee this afternoon?"

"I don't know. I've got shit to do. I've got to go. I'll talk to you later."

"I'm really sorry, you know. I…"

"Say bye."

"Bye, Sprout," he said, the sad and pathetic quality of the words ringing in his ears after the beep of the call ending.

An hour later Cody went for a walk in the park along the Mississippi, wearing a backpack carrying two water bottles of wine mixed with water. It was a warm and clear February day, and the Mississippi churned along in great whirls of brown water. The paved walkways of the new park passed through immaculately landscaped beds. Bikers passed intermittently. The gardens gave way to a narrower path between the railroad tracks and the river. A few years ago there had been no trace of the park that existed now. He remembered one late summer night when he had climbed over the levee wall with his friend Lauren, the poet, to skinny dip in the river. Now everything was clean and orderly, and park police zipped by regularly in golf carts, quick to admonish anyone who wandered off the path.

Cody paused to take a sip from his water bottle, and looked out across the river at the point of Algiers, so named historically because, like Algiers in relation to France, it stood across a great body of water. Oh, how the mighty are fallen, he thought. It was a statement that passed through his mind regularly. He put his backpack across his shoulders and resumed his walk. But what had he fallen from? His life as an adult stretched before him like the river, inscrutable, opaque, always flowing.

He remembered the first week after graduating college, after family members had left and the excitement of the event had given way to the reality. At last, he had been free to do whatever he wanted, and yet he'd felt like some leaf that had floated for miles through rapids and waterfalls only to find itself abruptly spinning slow circles in a dark mire. Amara and Sara. The Lily and the Orchid. And now, Sprout. All the bright lights he'd chased to escape the darkness, the fireflies promising a way to the sea. Each one was unique. Each one had pressed her world into his own and made his life a little better, and a little worse. After all, nothing could be more pathetic than a man in love. Through all of it these women and his experiences with them seemed the most meaningful ones of his life. He strived to piece it all together. If he could see it from the right perspective, it might all make sense.

THE NAZARENE

On the day of Sprout's birthday Cody went for a long walk along the river with his guitar. He found an empty bench and sat down to play. He remembered that first afternoon together eight years ago when he'd sat there with Amara, telling her about the flatboatmen of New Orleans. He felt like one of those flatboatmen now who had spent all of his money, staring at the Mississippi out of luck and out of love. That was the time to make the long walk back up the Mississippi to wherever you'd started from. Where could you go though when New Orleans was your only home?

Cody played the song he'd started writing while camping with Sprout. It had a minor chromatic, gypsy sort of melody. He still couldn't figure out the lyrics. After awhile he noticed a group of about eight people standing near him, perhaps a family judging from the range of ages among them. They talked together and occasionally glanced at him. Eventually they approached with smiles.

"We couldn't help but notice that unlike all the other musicians down here you're just playing for yourself."

"I was trying to finish a song."

"Ah, well we're here in New Orleans looking for people who could use a little help. And we saw you sitting here, and thought maybe you could use some people to pray with you."

Cody looked around at the smiling faces full of good intentions.

"I'm sure you all are good people. I'm not really religious though, and I think there are a lot of other people around here who could use your help more than me."

He watched them depart. They really did seem like good people, and he was certainly in a bad state, but after all he'd done how could he start praying now? What sympathy could this Borgia ever hope to receive? He remembered his last conversation with Sprout, saying, "I thought that maybe it was going to be like the other times. You'd be mad at me for awhile but then we'd make up."

"I know, I'm sorry," she'd said. "I guess I like sex."

For a time he had been the young man on the silver scooter fresh from Italy, driving the streets of his beloved city to this or that bar. He remembered the many times he drove down Esplanade Avenue singing out the theme of Dvorak's New World Symphony. What was it Nietzsche had written, something about how the thought of suicide had consoled him on many a difficult night?

That evening, Cody rose from his bed and walked into the kitchen where his housemate was cooking. He mumbled a greeting and from the corner of his eye waited to be sure his housemate was not looking at him. He took a large kitchen knife from the counter and walked back toward his bedroom carrying the knife next to his thigh. In his room he set the knife on the refrigerator and began looking up how to stab oneself in the heart. He thought about how, at the end of our days, for her to have come into his life unexpectedly and he hadn't even had the grace to be grateful.

When he walked out of the house the sidewalk and streets were still wet from the rain, and the air was heavy with the cool weight of it. He rounded the block and proceeded to the St. Roch cemetery. He hung his backpack on one of the pikes as he climbed over the gate. As he'd done many times he walked around the perimeter of the cemetery, on the path between the wall crypts and the elaborate mausoleums. The names and dates of the departed trickled through his consciousness.

At last having circled around he cut into the interior of the cemetery to where it opened into a small square in the center. He stood before the statue of the Nazarene, dropping his bag and removing one of his water bottles. He drank until it was empty, and stared up at the gentle face carved out of stone.

He reached down into the backpack and removed the kitchen knife, placing the tip of it between the third and fourth ribs on the left side of his chest. The cold brutal tip of it stood against his skin. He looked up at the statue and breathed a deep breath. He hesitated. It was going to hurt so much. And then in an angry blink it was done, the knife was in him and he was falling to the ground. He watched the blood pooling on the dark stones and wanted to remove the knife, but he could not move his arms. And then he was dead.

EARTHWARD: A NOVELLA

"Just as petals fall from drying garlands, which you can see aimlessly swimming in wine-bowls are we lovers, who now puff up our chests, but perhaps tomorrow the fateful day will shut us down."

- Propertius Sextus

I

It was early summer in Central Oregon and to the west the peaks of the Cascade Mountains were still white with patches of the winter's snow. The mountains gave way to pine-covered hills and then to the tan plains of the high desert stretching far into the east. The land changed quickly and the Deschutes River flowed right through the center. It ran swift and clear from the deep waters of Little Lava Lake through forests, swamps, and meadows, growing stronger and darkening as it wandered through desert canyons all the way to the broad reaches of the Columbia.

On the banks of the Deschutes, across from the lava beds, I stood and looked upstream to where the river curved past a meadow. I watched it flow slowly past the grassy banks, billowing farther out in the deep green of the current. Across the river, rough mounds of obsidian burned in the afternoon light. The lava flow formed an island that split the river below the city and it was rumored to hold many small lakes. There were no bridges and for most of the island's length the river was too wild to gain access. But here the current slowed and across the river a small stream curled away into the reeds.

I had come to the river after three weeks that had passed like a rainy night when the steady downfall makes it feel quieter than silence. I did not mind the rain, but rather the rhythm that never varied. I was looking for a break in the storm when the sun streams down through the parting clouds and the sound of distant thunder rumbles through the air. For a long time I had been looking for something to hold up against the days that passed more quickly with every year. I had left Oregon two years before in search of it, living first in New Orleans and then in Italy. In those two years away the memory of the land had never left me. There had been many mornings when I woke with the fragrant scent of juniper and the sound of quick flowing streams in my mind. But as I walked beside the river I still had not felt the old connection to the land. I knew it was alright to feel differently about the places from my past. Still, it was difficult to let go of an idea that had grown more powerful through absence.

At the edge of the shore I removed my shirt and shoes. Across the river the stream curled away into the reeds like an unanswered question. I stepped into the water. The chill of the river's source in the alpine lakes numbed my legs and reached up to my thighs. I took a few deep breaths and tried to push away the thought of the cold. I dove into the water and the shock ran through the darkness of my shut eyes driving me to the surface. I came up breathing hard and struggled on through the current. The bank rushed by and it looked like I would glide on past the stream but then I came out of the main current into an eddy and my feet dug into the muddy bottom. I reached the shore and collapsed in the warm grass.

The reeds were thick around the stream and I let the sun warm my body before I waded back into the water. I followed the stream as it twisted through the reeds into a narrow canyon. Slowly a path of solid earth formed along the stream and I climbed out to walk alongside beneath the shade of aspen trees. The cliffs that enclosed the stream began to widen until I reached a series of thick willows. I bent down and pushed through the clinging branches. Where the branches ended the water of a lake began. It was a clear, shallow lake enclosed by sheer cliffs. On the far side of the lake a waterfall poured over the cliff into the water.

I sat against a tree and watched a red-tailed hawk circle above me. I closed my eyes and almost immediately I saw the cobbled streets of Rome in the springtime with the sunlight falling across the stones and the white walls of the buildings. Since my return the memory of Italy had filled my thoughts the way a good book helps to pass a rainy night. I remembered one day in early fall when I had gone to the baths of Caracalla with Laura, an Italian who studied at the American University in Rome. We had met through a friend and when I told her I liked to sketch she promised to take me to a good place. One week later we sat in the large grass field of the ancient Circus Maximus facing the ruins. It was a warm day and I worked steadily only stopping to remove my shirt. After a good hour I stood and walked over to see Laura's drawing. She asked me to help her stand because her legs were asleep. I reached down and pulled her up and I could feel the length of her body pressed against mine and her hands on my bare shoulders. She looked up at me and smiled, saying "my legs weren't really asleep." The memory had come to symbolize everything I loved about Italy, how the presence of the ancient ruins somehow heightened your resolve to live every moment to its fullest. But the memory was growing thin through repetition and I felt sick at the thought that I was living almost solely off of memories.

I opened my eyes and for the first time in weeks Italy slipped away from my thoughts. I seemed to notice for the first time how the waterfall poured down into the lake and I thought about the journey of this small stream all the way to the ocean only to return as rainfall. I stood and headed back along the stream to the river where a charter raft full of tourists passed by. When the raft disappeared around the next bend of the river I dove again into the cold water and swam across. On the other side I pulled on my clothes and walked down the trail to my car. I climbed into the seat of my old Isuzu Trooper and drove down the twisting gravel road to the highway.

As I drove the pine trees slowly gave way to homes and then to the ski shops and new craftsman-style homes of the city. Near the park I crossed the river and continued up along the old homes dating to the milling days of the city. The park was full of people playing Frisbee and walking their dogs beside the slow rolling waters of Mirror Pond. I turned on Bond Street and watched the people milling about in the art galleries, coffee shops and bars. I could remember when hardly anyone went downtown, but everything had changed dramatically in the course of the last ten years. Ten minutes later I parked at the head of a driveway on the edge of the river canyon.

Jules lived in a two-story house of pine and cedar with windows that looked out on the Deschutes. It was built deep in the canyon on the banks of the river before regulations outlawed construction so close to the water. I followed the winding gravel road as it dropped down the slope of the canyon into a small driveway. I stepped onto the deck of the house and knocked on the door as a light breeze passed through the chimes on the porch. The door opened and Jules said with a big smile:

"What the hell took you so long? We've got drinking to do."

"Well, let's get started."

I followed Jules across the wood floors of the sunlit house. A childhood bone disease had stunted his growth and for the first twelve years of his life he had been incapable of walking unaided. When he finally could walk it was with a laborious stagger. He had short sandy hair and an oval face with large eyes that always reminded me of an owl.

"Beer?" he offered.

"Sure."

"Let's go out by the river."

We walked out on the deck and I looked across the grass and pine trees to the granite cliffs on the far side of the river. We sat down on a series of boulders on the edge of the river and drank our beers. I watched the water flow around the polished boulders as the late afternoon sun reflected off the water.

"Summer is finally here," I said.

"It's been summer for a while now."

"I know, but somehow I couldn't see past Italy. All I could think about was the sun shining in the streets brighter than anything I saw here, until today."

"Sounds like a revelation."

"Nothing as dramatic as that. I just went for a walk along the river and as I was sitting beneath a tree on the lava island I woke up and remembered I was home. I mean, really felt like I was home."

"You're turning into a mystic. By the way, how did you get across the river?"

"I swam."

"You crazy bastard, it's freezing."

"I know. Invigorating."

He laughed and took a long sip from his beer.

"So what's the plan for tonight?" I asked.

"Lydia is coming over in a little while."

"What's she like? I didn't know her in High School."

"You left for New Orleans right when I became friends with her. She's really brilliant."

"And beautiful, as I recall."

"That too, although I'm not sure she's interested in me that way."

"Too bad."

"Don't get any ideas, Casanova. I care for her too much to let her fall into your hands."

"What's wrong with me? Better a friend than a stranger."

"Bullshit, you're too cavalier to fall in love."

"I could fall in love…with the right woman."

"For a week maybe. What happened with that woman in Italy?"

"Laura?"

"Yes, tell me about lovely Laura."

"Well, she was Italian. And she had a villa off the coast and a leopard."

"A fucking leopard?"

"Yeah, right out of Scarface. But he was dead when I arrived. All that remained was a large cage and a sign with his name."

"Were you in love with her?" Jules asked.

"No, not really. She was pretty and interesting. But I wasn't really in love with her."

"See what I mean? Only you could somehow not fall in love with a rich Italian woman who owned a villa and a leopard."

"You might have a point. But for the sake of optimism I'll hold out against it. Want another beer?"

"Sure. Actually, why don't you make us some drinks?"

I walked up to the house and returned with two glasses of whiskey and water.

We sat there as the air cooled and the sun dipped behind the rim of the canyon. I looked at the rocks where Jules and I had played as kids. We had been friends then in the easy way that children make friends with anyone of sympathetic imagination. It was not until high school that we really became friends. The change had been gradual but there was one night that stood out above the rest. We had all gone camping on Lake Wickiup. It was late at night and everyone else had gone to sleep. Jules and I walked through the woods along the shore. We were out of beer so Jules suggested we raid a few ice chests in the other camps. We filled our hands with beer and set off onto the lake in an old boat. The whole time it felt like something had changed, as if we were joined by awareness of how childhood had slipped away and of how it was good to go back to it now and then.

"Damn Jules, wouldn't it be great to just jump into your car and head out east through the desert all the way to Montana?"

"And do what exactly?"

"Live."

"Well, of course I'd love to, but I have to start working. Besides, I just got back from school. I need a break from life."

I had never heard Jules respond with hesitation to that kind of question.

"What about life in the big sense? Remember when we were kids and life was going to be a big adventure. But then it didn't quite turn out that way, did it?"

"That's ironic coming from a nineteen year old who just spent a year living in Italy and dating a woman with a leopard. I think that's just part of growing up. You don't see the world realistically as a kid."

"What if the only time you see the world realistically is when you're young, before the world lays its claims and obligations on you?"

"When I was a kid I was certain that I would be a paleontologist. And you were going to be an archaeologist like Indiana Jones. What happened to that?"

"A change of heart."

"Exactly. You learned that being an archaeologist meant digging up potsherds all day in the blazing sun instead of globe-trotting and making love to beautiful, exotic women. The same goes for how we see life."

"But what if all those promises you made to yourself as a kid make a difference in your life now? I've got a feeling that everything I imagined as a kid will haunt me if I don't live up to it."

"Why does life have to make sense that way? Billions of people have come and gone on this earth who never left the small world of their home town and its surroundings. They lived and died and were forgotten. What makes you think there is so much more than that?"

"Just a feeling. Come on now, you're a Nietzsche fan: 'Live dangerously: build your cities on the slopes of Vesuvius.' You have to feel that to really understand it."

"Well, I can follow the philosophy. But in terms of what you're saying about your life, I'm not sure that I agree."

"But philosophy is life."

"What if there are no answers to these questions? You live your life and even at the end you may not know anything for sure…"

We heard a voice from the house and we turned around to see Lydia walking down the gravel path to the rocks. I had not seen her in years. She walked with an easy, measured gait holding her gaze on us and a slight smile on her lips. Her tight black shirt matched her long hair and her jeans revealed a slim figure with emphasis in all the right places. She sat down on the boulder next to Jules and glanced briefly at me with her dark eyes.

"Hi Lydia," I said.

"Hi."

She turned to Jules, "What are you boys talking about?"

"Life…in the big sense preferred by him and the small one without sense that I prefer."

"Sounds kind of senseless."

"I think you're probably right," Jules said. "Would you like a drink?"

"Absolutely. I'll go make it. Do you need another?"

"Please."

"Careful Jules, you'll be of no use to her if you're wasted."

Lydia stood and said over her shoulder as she walked to the house:

"What makes you think I need him for anything?"

I laughed to myself as Jules eyed me and said: "You like her, don't you?"

"Well, she's a beautiful girl."

"Yes she is…," he paused for a moment.

"Back to our conversation…I think a lot of people feel the way I do but over time they find a way to forget about it, or they find ways to distract themselves. You would probably say it's just growing up, but what if there's a good and natural reason for feeling like things aren't quite right in your life, especially when there are moments that suggest something better?"

"You should see what Lydia thinks about it."

Lydia walked back and sat down next to Jules. She looked slowly from Jules to me.

"Okay, what's going on?" she asked.

"Go ahead, tell Lydia about it," Jules said.

"I was talking about how as a child I had so many ideas about the way life would be and suddenly I find that I'm nineteen and the world is very different from how I expected it to be. Take today, for example. Since I got back from Italy a few weeks ago I've been living in a kind of stupor. I was not really miserable or unhappy, but I felt unsatisfied, like something was missing. And then today I went to the river and swam across to the big island. I followed a little stream all the way to a hidden lake surrounded by cliffs and the sun was shining down and for a moment it all felt right, like I'd found whatever was missing before. It was like I could see the world with fresh eyes again. The point I was trying to make is that although as kids we may not see the world realistically, there is something from our childhood that we need to hold onto because it makes sense of the world in a strange way. Do you know what I mean?"

I looked at Lydia and felt uncomfortable under her intense gaze.

"Where did you go on the river?" she asked.

"On the Deschutes by Lava River Island…"

"By the Indian Shelter?"

"Yes. You've been there?"

"My father used to take me there as a kid," she said.

"It's a beautiful place, isn't it?"

91

"Yes."

"Well, we could go there sometime, if you want."

"That would be fun."

"I'm getting cold out here," Jules said. "Let's go inside."

We began walking up to the house. I stayed outside a moment to look at the sky as the purple spread from the east. I could feel the alcohol setting in. It was always the same when it first set in, the feeling that anything was possible and would probably happen that very night. I wondered why Jules wanted me to stay away from Lydia. She seemed to have felt what I was saying. As I walked back inside Jules was speaking in a loud voice.

"What I mean is that it's ridiculous to think that life has to live up to the ideals of childhood. You don't believe that, do you?"

"No, not that it has to live up to those ideals exactly," Lydia said. "But maybe something from our childhood influences how we gain enjoyment and meaning from the world."

"That's all I mean, Jules," I said.

"Oh bullshit. I can hardly walk and you're telling me how your life doesn't measure up to your childhood dreams."

"Jules, you know I don't mean it like that."

He sat down in a chair and looked straight ahead. I walked to the door and opened it.

"Look, Jules, I've got to get going. I'm sorry. You know I didn't mean anything like that."

"I just need time to cool off. I'll see you tomorrow," he said.

"What?"

"The party tomorrow night out by Sisters. I'll see you when we go out there."

"Right."

I closed the door and began walking up the driveway. I heard the door open and turned to see Lydia walking after me.

"I'm sorry about that," she said.

"It's alright. I'm used to Jules. And he has a point."

"Look, would you be interested in doing something tomorrow? I know you guys are going to the party tomorrow night, but maybe we could do something in the morning?"

"Sure. I'd love to."

"Here's my number. Call me tomorrow."

She turned and jogged back down the driveway and through the door into the house. I watched the door for a moment and then headed back up the driveway to my car. I drove east past the rows of subdivision homes until only a long narrow road stretched on through the moonlit fields. I reached my driveway and drove down along the canal and parked.

It was a small house on eight acres of land and in the winter the winds howled across the plains and shook the frame of the house. I had lived there for most of my childhood and spent my days roaming through the fields and exploring the caves on the adjoining properties. In the summer you could hear the sound of crickets and frogs all through the night and the winters were always very cold and windy. I could still remember how it felt as a child eating breakfast on a winter morning when it was dark outside and the fire gleamed through the glass door of the woodstove. Moving the blinds to one side I could see the snow fallen over night piled on the railings of the deck and the porch light made the snow crystals shimmer across the lawn. I ate my cereal and listened to the moaning of the wind in the trees. And sometimes I felt an empty space open in my stomach, even though I was eating, and I became aware of myself as a child, aware of my consciousness and the way the wind made me feel and I thought it was strange, but then it was gone and soon the sun spread its light across the quiet snow-covered fields and I caught the bus to school in front of our house.

I walked up the stairs of the deck into the darkness of the house. In the study I sat down and picked up a worn notebook. I wanted to write something about the day's experience and I tried to remember all the feelings and images of walking along the river and how it felt to find the hidden lake. Soon my thoughts drifted to Lydia and I imagined her standing in the gravel driveway looking at me.

The heavy steps of my father echoed down the hall as he walked to the study. He opened the door and looked in, a large man with brown hair and eyes.

"Reading again?"

"Yeah."

"Can I talk to you for a moment?"

"Sure."

He walked in and sat down in a chair with the slow muscularity of a bear.

"What did you do today?" he asked.

"I went to the Deschutes River by Lava Island Falls and walked around. Then I went over to Jules' house."

"How is he doing?"

"Pretty good. He just returned from school."

"Good. I just wanted to make sure everything was alright. You've been kind of quiet lately. Is everything alright?"

"Sure."

"Are you going to start looking for a job soon?"

"Yeah, I will. But what should I do?"

"You could try landscaping. Or you could work at G.I. Joe's again. The important thing is to make money for when you start school in the fall."

I felt myself trying to imagine my father's life. For a long time I had not wanted to be like him. He had spent the last twenty years of his life going to work each day, first as a salesman and then as a realtor. For twenty years he had known nothing but offices and clients. You couldn't hold it against him, but it was hard not to. I liked to think that at some point in his life things had been different, that at some point he had known poetry in life. But he did not read books.

"Dad, when were you happiest in your life?"

"I don't know. I'm happy now."

He was quiet for a moment as he looked at me and smiled a little.

"I remember being pretty happy as a kid when we lived on the river in Roseburg. We had a boat with a little motor on the back and I used to cruise up and down the river. And then we used to ride bikes all over the place. Remember the swimming hole I showed you? We used to ride our bikes there every day in the summer."

He watched me silently and then said:

"Are you happy?"

"Sort of, but the point isn't necessarily to be happy, is it?"

"It helps. I would hate to think that you are unhappy."

"Well, I'm not, really."

"I think you just need to fall in love. I think it would be good for you."

"Sure, but you can't decide to fall in love. It just happens, right? Isn't that what makes it special?"

"Yes, but you can be more open to it."

"How?"

"I'm not exactly sure. I think I went through what you're going through when I was in college. And then I met your mother."

"What was that like?"

"She was so much younger than me. After I quit college I lived with my parents and she lived next door. She used to sunbathe in the front yard. I asked her out eventually."

He was silent for a moment, and then he said:

"You know, I've never really told you this, but part of the reason we divorced was that I was never really in love with your mother."

I looked at him silently and he continued:

"We were just dating and then she started having trouble at home. I helped her out of that, but she was dead set on marrying me. Don't get me wrong, we were happy together for awhile and having you and your sister was wonderful, but when I married your mother I wasn't really in love with her."

"Why are you telling me this?"

He looked uncomfortable but went on:

"I just want you to be more open to falling in love and meeting different people. I wish I had been more open when I was your age. It's a good idea to discover what you like in other people, and to do that you have to take some chances."

He said he was going to bed and I listened as his steps grew dimmer until there was only silence. I sat in the chair thinking about Lydia and my father's words and wondered what the hell to make of both. I looked down at the notebook in my lap and tossed it aside. I was too distracted to write. I began to grow tired and I walked into my room and crawled into the bed. The moon illuminated the grove

95

of junipers in the backyard and I thought about all the nights I had looked out at the stars and thought about many things before going to sleep. Sometimes I tried to think about eternity and what it meant to live forever as my mother had told me that after death we would all go on living in heaven. Such thinking usually ended with a knot in my stomach as there is nothing quite so unnerving as really trying to imagine eternity.

Jesus, I thought, what the hell could you do with it all? When you really thought about it this moment was no different than the others. You were older now but as you lay there in your old bed and thought back over it you knew that it was all just as vital and real as when you lived it: the memories surging through you in no distinct order, moving swiftly from a warm summer day spent digging in the mud as a child to catching the bus in the dark when you were thirteen to walking by the Castel Sant' Angelo a few months before. Maybe Jules was right. You lived in spite of yourself and no matter what you did the fullness of it could not be suppressed. Images of Italy and Oregon grew more vivid and then began to merge together and I knew I was falling asleep. I tried to stay aware as long as possible but sleep, as it always does, pushed away self-awareness even before it fully set in. And then I slept and I dreamed I was in the old house out in the country but Laura was with me although sometimes she was also Lydia.

II

I woke up late the next morning and walked outside onto the deck. The day was coming along well and the air still smelled like the wet grass in early morning mixed with the bittersweet scent of juniper. I looked across the fields of green alfalfa and yellow cheatgrass and then west to the peaks of the mountains. It would be a good day. It was always good to wake up and find the skies clear. I walked across the grass along the old fire-scarred juniper fence posts to the small pond. A rickety dock led into the water. I walked to the end of the dock and watched the sleek, dark shadows of the bass holding close to the pile of branches in the center. They reminded me of the brown trout in the pools of Paulina Creek. I walked back to the house and picked up the phone. Lydia sounded half asleep when she answered.

"Hello?"

"Hi Lydia."

"Hi, what are you doing?"

"Nothing. Did you have any ideas for something to do today?"

"Not really. Don't you have some special places you can show me?"

"There is one, but you can't tell anybody about it."

"Why not?"

"You'll see."

An hour later I picked up Lydia and we drove south around the red cinder cone of Lava Butte. The pine trees grew sparser until only plains and farmlands stretched to the horizon. We turned off the highway toward Newberry Caldera, a lone peak above the plains. The winding road climbed steadily and the pine trees returned as we ascended. We took a dirt road that wound along the top of a ridge and the plains spread out below us with the Cascade Mountains to the far west. I parked the car in a turnout and we followed a thin trail down into a canyon. A few years before a fire had ripped through the area leaving only the scattered stalks of trees, burnt and limbless. The land had recovered quickly though and now waist-high pines dotted the canyon and manzanita bushes nearly swallowed the trail.

At the bottom of the canyon the stream ran gently past large grey boulders and grass. The water gleamed with a bronze tint from the tan rocks of the river bed. We followed a path along the stream until we arrived at a log dam where three waterfalls poured into a deep pool.

"Here we are," I said.

"It's beautiful. How did you find it?"

"Exploring, back in high school."

I took off my shirt and waded into the pool. The water was surprisingly warm and I leaned up against a flat boulder. Lydia took off her shorts and pulled her shirt over her head revealing a black swimsuit. As she waded into the water I tried not to stare at her full breasts and the smooth, pale olive of her skin.

"I can't believe how warm it is," she said.

"Come over into the falls."

The water poured down on us and we swam around in the pool. I dove under the water and swam right past Lydia, gently brushing my hand against her leg and then swimming off to surface by the falls.

"I think a fish just swam past my leg," she said with a sly grin.

"Must have been a big one."

We swam around for a while and then we climbed out and set down a blanket to sit on. I pulled a bottle of wine out of my backpack and some bread and cheese. The sun warmed the blanket and the grass and illuminated the tan rocks of the riverbed. I felt almost dizzy with the joy of it. It was good to see the old area again. As a teenager I had spent many summer days walking along the stream and fishing. Often I had imagined bringing a girl there to swim in the pool and share the beauty of the place with me.

"You came prepared," Lydia said with a laugh.

I opened the bottle and poured some into the glasses.

"Jules was telling me about you last night," she said.

"I can't imagine it was anything good after what happened."

"He cooled off after a while. He really admires you. He said you were out of control as a kid and raised hell in class but the teachers still liked you. According to Jules you're really smart but you try not to show it."

"I don't know about that. Jules was always the intellectual."

"And you were the adventurer, I take it?"

"I wanted to be an adventurer. How did you become friends with Jules?"

"We had English class together, but we never talked. Then one night at a party he came up to me looking a bit drunk and said 'what do you think about Coleridge?' We'd just read "Rime of the Ancient Mariner" in class and I told him I liked Coleridge but I really loved Keats. He looked at me as if I was his long lost sister and hugged me right there. Then we started hanging out a little and he showed me some of his poetry."

"What did you think of it?"

"I liked it. I know Jules is intelligent, but sometimes his poetry tries too hard to seem smart, rather than really saying something. I love Jules, as a friend, but he's very young in some ways."

"It's hard to say, Jules can act deceptively simple sometimes."

"Yes," she said.

"I was wondering about what you said last night, about how you used to go with your father to Lava Island Falls."

"Yeah, that was around the time my parents were divorcing. We used to walk down there to the Indian shelter and talk about what was happening in the family."

"How old were you?"

"About eleven."

"I was the same age when my parents divorced."

"Was it hard on you?"

"At the time it was, but not anymore. How was it for you?"

99

"It was pretty bad. I never really thought my family would get a divorce. I thought it only happened to troubled families. Hah. And then when it started I didn't know how to take it."

I remembered the night my own parents had separated. Perhaps they had been separated for a long time before that but I always remembered the night I left home with my mother. The rain was falling and the drops ran down the windshield as if all of nature felt as I did. We pulled away from the house and I watched it grow smaller through the back window until it disappeared but I kept on looking. We lived in my grandmother's house and at night I sometimes imagined that my father would stand on the street-corner drunk and shout up at the house. It had been the first time the world had seemed truly irredeemable. I wondered what it had been like for Lydia She looked at me with her steady gaze and said:

"This might be kind of a personal question, but why did you move to New Orleans your senior year?"

"Remember what I was saying last night about staying true to some part of your childhood?"

"Yes."

"Well, going to New Orleans felt like the right thing to do in that sense. It seemed like the dangerous thing to do."

"Dangerous?"

"Well, not really dangerous, but risky. Most people wouldn't have done it and that was part of the appeal. I wanted to take a chance. It was all kind of symbolic for me. I had this feeling that if I waited too long to make some sort of risky decision then I probably never would. I was afraid my life would just roll on continuously and I would never be able to look back on a part of it and say, 'I did that, I made that happen. And now it's mine.' It was silly in some ways, but I can't say that I regret it. You know, it's all so strange, life. Last night my father told me that when he married my mother he wasn't in love with her. She was really young when they met and he felt forced into marrying her. Then he tells me that I need to fall in love. Jesus, I just don't understand any of it."

"Do you ever feel like our parents let us down? They grew up in the most idealistic time and then it's like they all copped out."

100

"Yeah, I know what you mean. A part of me thinks it's just part of society or getting older. You kind of lose that edgy boldness you have when you're young and maybe there's no avoiding it. As you get older more and more claims are attached to you. But it sure feels like it could have been different, although I wonder if my father ever even knew what I'm feeling now. I always wanted to be different than him, more dangerous, more alive. I wanted my life to mean more than bills and the next possession. It feels like it could be different."

"I think it could be."

I looked at her and saw the way her dark hair still wet from the water fell down her back. Her black eyes stared steadily into my own and I felt a quivering ache pass through me as of a night when the stars shine so brightly that it almost hurts you with the aimless desire it puts into your soul. But this desire was specific and as I looked at her it seemed like she too wanted it. The wine and the feeling conspired to push away all hesitation and I leaned forward to kiss her and she responded with a long, deep kiss that led to the blanket and finally to our clothes coming off and ended with the two of us supine on the blanket and the sun warm on our skin.

The sound of the stream and the occasional bird chirping were more noticeable now, and I took a long sip from my glass of wine and thought of nothing. Lydia leaned over my chest and I ran my hand over the smooth skin of her back and thought about how good it was to have her there. We stayed by the pool for most of the afternoon swimming occasionally and then warming up on the blanket until the sun began to sink and the shade of the trees moved over our spot. We made love again with one half of the blanket pulled over us and when it ended the air was cold against our wet skin. We put on our clothes drove up the road to the lake.

It was a deep crater lake and all that remained of the former volcano was a jagged peak golden in the late sun. The peak stood on one side of the lake and there was a lodge by the water and cabins painted red stretched down along the shore. A dock led out into the lake and we walked down the rough pine planks and looked down into the clear water where the carp gathered in schools. There were also brown trout in the lake and large schools of kokanee, a species of landlocked salmon, in the deepest parts. We walked back to the lodge and into the restaurant. Pictures of trophy brown trout held by grinning fishermen hung on the walls. A woman began to build a fire in the woodstove because even in the summer the temperature usually dropped over thirty degrees at night. The smell of wood-smoke grew stronger and it was good to think about all the feelings contained in the scent of burning pine. Outside the window the sky grew purple to the east and the looming peak was orange in the light of the setting sun.

We looked at the menus for a minute and then I looked up at Lydia and saw that her face had lost its usual calm.

"What's wrong?" I asked.

She looked up from her menu and it was clear that she was bothered.

"I'm worried about Jules," she said. "I don't know what he's going to think about all of this."

"What do you mean?"

"I think he's in love with me."

"He said yesterday that he didn't think you loved him."

"Well, I don't, not in the way he likes me. He's a good friend, and we've been friends for awhile. But you're his best friend and I don't know how he's going to take it."

"Maybe I shouldn't go to the party tonight. I'd forgotten all about it."

"No, you should go. You need to tell him."

"God, what the hell am I going to say to him? 'Jules, I had sex with Lydia Sorry pal.' Yesterday he told me to stay away from you."

"Why did he say that?"

"He wasn't real clear. It's almost like he knew something might happen. I'm such an asshole. I completely forgot about it. It might be easier if we're together at the party. Do you want to go with me?"

"I could, but I can't stay for long. I have to help my father tomorrow morning, but I could drive you out there. Jules will probably leave before we get back, anyway."

"It might be better that way. Do you really think he'll be angry about it?"

"I don't know. I told him a long time ago that I just wanted to be friends but I think he's always hoped for something more."

The waitress came and we ordered. Soon two plates of fresh kokanee were on the table. I liked the fine salmon flavor of the kokanee but we had to eat quickly and soon we were on the road back to Bend.

* * *

It was dark by the time we reached the large, lodge-style home on the slope of a hill outside of Sisters. The sound of a bass thumped loudly from the house. A raised deck extended from the driveway to the door and tall windows looked out from the front. We stepped inside, removed our shoes and walked on the tan wood floors into the living room. A few people danced to the music. Jules sat on the couch absorbed in the music. After a moment he saw us and walked over.

"Hey guys, come here."

Jules led us to the kitchen where a few bottles of liquor sat on the counter. I mixed a Jack and coke and we walked out onto the large back deck. The smell of marijuana drifted on the breeze.

"Hey, Baker."

I looked toward one of the tables on the corner of the deck and saw a couple of acquaintances from High School. They stood up and walked over.

"Hey man, you grew your hair out," said the first one.

"Yeah, you're a damn hippie," said the other.

"You want to smoke?" asked the first.

"Nah, I'm alright."

They walked inside in search of participants. We sat down at the empty table but Jules left after a minute saying he wanted to hear the music better.

"Well, he hasn't said anything about us coming here together," I said.

"He actually looks pretty happy."

"Maybe he doesn't care."

"He must be stoned. Anyways, I should probably get going. Are you going to be alright here? You don't look too excited."

"I'll be fine. I just have to warm up to the party."

We stood up and walked back through the house and out to her car. We said goodbye and then she drove off down the driveway and I walked back into the house. As I entered I heard the familiar opening riff to Jimi Hendrix's "Hey Joe" and walked into the living room to see Jules sprawled on the ground writhing in ecstasy. A few people watched with amusement, but most seemed oblivious. I walked over beside him and looked down:

"What the hell are you on, Jules?"

"E."

"Ecstasy?"

"That's right."

I sat back on the couch and took a sip of my drink. I had known Jules to smoke weed occasionally, but had never seen him take ecstasy. He continued his snake dance on the floor. After a few minutes he tired and climbed on the couch beside me.

"I have something for you," Jules said and then reached into his pocket and removed a pill in plastic wrap.

"What is it?"

"Adderall. Don't have any more E."

"I don't want to be up all night."

"Oh for Christ's sake would you just mellow out and have a good time. I'm high as a kite and the least you can do is sympathize by way of chemical proximity."

I laughed and then I swallowed the pill and waited for the effect. Jules went on excitedly:

"You know something? I'm sorry about how I acted last night. I do think you were right. I just wasn't in the mood for it then. I knew it was going to happen with you and Lydia. I just wasn't ready to accept it."

"You know Jules, I am sorry."

"Don't apologize. There's nothing to apologize for. She's great. You two probably had a wonderful day together."

"Jules, why did you take E?"

"I needed to stir things up a bit. I just got out of school, remember?"

We sat listening to the music for awhile but then I began to feel the adderall speeding up my thoughts and I felt like going outside.

"Jules, let's go get some air."

We walked out on the back deck and sat down at one of the tables. Jules tapped his foot restlessly to the beat and looked around.

"Matt, I've got to tell you that part of the reason I was so sensitive last night is that I've been working on a story about two guys who are in love with the same woman. What happened last night was eerily similar to the story."

"Hasn't that been done before Jules?"

"Well, yes, but the story is just a vehicle, a way into the dream, you know?"

"How far along are you?"

"Pretty far."

A woman walked out onto the deck and sat down in a chair near Jules. She was an attractive woman with dark hair and from the redness of her eyes she appeared to be stoned. Jules leaned over and introduced himself.

"What do you do?" she asked.

"I'm a poet."

"No you're not."

"Yes, I am," he said.

"Recite one, then."

"Right now?"

"Yes."

"Okay. Especially for you: 'She walks in beauty like the night / Of cloudless climes and starry skies; /And all that's best of dark and bright, / Meet in her aspect and her eyes...'"

Jules recited the whole damn poem and never once moved his intense gaze from her eyes.

"Oh my god, you wrote that?" she asked.

"Just for you."

"Where are you from?" she said and moved a little closer.

I stood up and walked to the kitchen to fix a drink. I filled a glass with Scotch and mixed in a little water. I had a feeling Jules would be occupied for the rest of the night and I needed something to slow me down. I walked back outside again and breathed the cool night air. It was a fine night and I walked down the stairs of the deck through the trees. It was clear enough to see the scattered sage bushes. I laughed to myself as I remembered Jules reciting Byron's poem. It was a new side to him although I had always felt he had it in him. There was something wonderful about seeing a friend take on a new dimension. Jules had been terrified of women for most of his life although he idealized them in his poetry. The ecstasy had something to do with it, of course, but I liked to think that the drug was only a final catalyst to something that had been growing for a long time.

I found an old juniper and sat with my back against the trunk. Hell of a day, I thought, and ran my hand through the dry, sandy dirt. It was not exactly beautiful, this land. But I had not really known that until later. For a long time it had been enough simply to look at the landscape and turn it into whatever I desired. And then later when I had learned to see its frailties and its rough, old man nature, it was still possible to think of it as an ancient land charged with wisdom. I saw those rolling plains and imagined its native guardians riding to the vital confluence of rivers, or to the sacred solitude of the desert mountain surrounded by raw obsidian. The land had the quiet, mystical soul of a sage or shaman, an old man with long hair and otherworldly eyes like the self-portrait Da Vinci drew in his last years, eyes that looked straight into you and revealed a desiring soul fastened to a dying animal...

The horses pounded across a dry plain kicking up dust. They drew closer and closer until I thought they would run me over and I could see the wild look in their eyes and the sweat pouring down their necks. I woke with a start and saw that the sun had risen. I stood and began walking with my head still humming and my stomach growling. I had not walked far in the night and soon I reached the back deck of the house where the door had been left open. In the living room Jules sat cross-legged by the speakers moving rhythmically from side to side as the music played softly.

"Jules, didn't you sleep?"

It took a moment for the question to register and then he swiveled around.

"No."

"Well, what happened with the girl?"

"It was so good I can't even describe it. Where did you go, Walt Whitman?"

"I wandered outside and fell asleep at the base of a tree."

"Typical. I'm getting hungry. You want to head back to town and eat?"

"Sure, but I'm still too damned tired to drive."

"I can drive. I've never been more alive and awake in my life."

"You sure?"

"Absolutely."

We walked outside to Jules' car. As we drove down the long asphalt driveway to the highway Jules put some music on and I felt myself growing sleepy. I shut my eyes and drifted with the music.

When I woke the dashboard appeared to have moved closer. I felt something wet on my head and then I saw the spider-web crack in the windshield. I looked over towards Jules. The steering wheel had been driven into his chest and blood oozed from his mouth.

"Jules, what the hell happened? Jules, are you alright?"

"I can't move."

"What?"

"I can't move. I can't feel anything."

I felt a wave pass through me like I might vomit and my eyes closed. I struggled to open them and looked back at Jules. Then hands reached into the car and I felt myself being pulled out of the windshield. I turned my head and saw Jules's car smashed and near it another car looked equally devastated.

"Get Jules, Jules," I shouted but then I was in a van moving down the highway and I felt tired again and my eyes closed.

The room was white: the sheets, the walls, and even the light through the window. I saw my father sitting in a chair at the opposite end of the small room. He stood and walked to the side of the bed.

"Dad, where's Jules?"

"You were in a car accident."

"Jules?"

"Jules died in the accident."

III

Jules fell asleep going sixty miles an hour down Highway 20. He crashed head on into another car going the opposite direction, killing the other driver almost instantly. In the weeks that followed many people visited me and offered their condolences. At the funeral I said hello to Lydia and then left after the services. That I had gained the love of Lydia only worsened my guilt over the death of Jules. For three weeks I stayed at home reading and thinking over the event. I became sensitive to all living things and saw transience in every plant and animal. I planted flowers and watered them religiously. Most of all I became obsessed with the idea of creating something to commemorate my fallen friend. Every day I played my guitar and tried to write a song about Jules. After three weeks I felt I had something and when I played it my father became teary-eyed.

Early one summer afternoon my father walked into the study where I sat in the old recliner with my guitar across my lap. He sat down in the chair across from me and spoke:

"Matt, I know how hard this has been. But you have to understand that this happens every day all over the world. I know it feels horrible, as if your life will never be the same. But it will. I know I've told about my friend Dave, the one who drove off the bridge and died. I know how it feels. But you have to get yourself together and keep living. Take this weekend off, but then on Monday I want you to start looking for a job."

He put his hand on my shoulder and then walked out. After a

while I stood and walked outside to the pond. I stood on the dock and looked into the water. Only a month ago I had stood there thinking of Lydia and the day we would have together. And Jules had been alive then.

A car came down the driveway and parked. A few of my old friends walked across the grass.

"Get your stuff, man, we're going camping."

"I'm not going."

"Come on man, you have to go. We're all going."

"I'm not in the mood."

"Matt," said a friend I had known since sixth grade. "We're doing this for Jules. It's in memory of him."

"Where are you going to camp?"

"On Wickiup, where we used to go."

"Okay," I said after a moment and then walked into the house. I grabbed my fishing pole and threw a pair of swimming shorts into a bag. I hesitated for a moment and then picked up my guitar. I was ready.

We drove southwest on the Cascade Lakes Highway passing around the volcanic dome of Mt. Bachelor. The steep summit of the South Sister came into view with the snow still clinging to its sides and beside it the red and brown geological layers of Broken Top jutted out of the earth. As we passed the clear emerald water of Devil's Lake I began to feel something inside me that I had not felt in weeks and I no longer felt hesitant about my decision. We drove for another forty-five minutes and pulled off onto a dirt road that led to the shore of Lake Wickiup.

The lake was a reservoir on the upper Deschutes River and through the summer its water level varied. As we pulled into the turnout by the shore I saw that the water was lower than usual and exposed an island in the center. We parked and began hauling our tents onto the smoothed-over patches of ground beneath the trees. Having put up the tents, we gathered by the cooler down on the sand of the shore. I had been friends with Steven, John, and Seton since middle school. I had often wondered what held the group of guys together. They were not friends in the way Jules had been a friend, but I always felt comfortable around them although as we grew older we had less in common. I figured that somehow in that anxious period of adolescence we had banded together for strength and though the situation had changed, the bonds remained.

"Let's start drinking," John said and opened the cooler.

"Always in a hurry," Steven said.

"No better time to start," John responded and opened a beer.

"Tara, Liz, and Lydia are supposed to come up later," Steven said and looked at me.

"Hey Matt, I heard you hooked up with Lydia," said Seton.

"Yeah. Anyone want to go fishing?"

"I'll go with you," Seton said.

We gathered up our fishing poles and a small tackle box and drove back to the main road. On the far end of the lake a bridge crossed the Deschutes where it entered the reservoir. I parked the car and we walked out along the railing of the bridge. I stared down into the water and saw a few fish in the shade of the bridge. After awhile I saw the dark shadows of the larger fish holding close to the sunken logs.

"I'm going to fish on the lake side," Seton said.

"Alright, I'm going upstream where the lively ones are."

I walked along the river bank away from the lake. The current quickened as I continued until I reached a fallen log that blocked the path. I walked down the length of the log to a large boulder. From the boulder I had room to lengthen my line behind me and cast to the far side of the river. I tied on a dry fly and began slowly moving the rod back and forth over my head extending line from the reel. My touch was rough at first but then I began to catch the rhythm of it and I remembered the pleasure of losing myself in the easy flow of casting. The fly settled on the swirling waters and floated on the current for a few seconds and then dipped below the water. I pulled up the rod drawing the fly out of the water and cast it back and forth over my head a few times to dry the fly. I set the fly down in about the same spot but still nothing struck.

I cast over my head and studied the opposite shore. On the far side there was a boulder and next to it a fallen tree extended into the

111

water. I set the fly down right next to the boulder and watched it float along the length of the fallen tree. The fish broke the water at the far end of the tree and swallowed the lure diving down and into the current and I set the hook hard and felt the rod tremble with the solid, throbbing weight of the fish. The fish leaped a few times, its sleek shimmering body arching through the air and splashing noisily into the water. I laughed aloud with the excitement and finally drew the fish in near the shore. It was a brown trout with small sharp teeth. I bent down to pick it up but it slipped through my fingers. Finally I caught the fish under the belly and raised it just above the water. I removed the hook and watched the fish dart back into the current.

I set down my pole and reclined on the boulder. I took off my shirt and felt the sun on my body and listened to the steady rush of the river. Eventually I slipped into a deep sleep and after an hour or two I woke to the sound of Seton's calls. I stood and walked back up along the bank to the bridge.

"How did you do?" Seton asked.

"I caught one, and then I just took a nap. How about you?"

"Nothing. You always were a good fisherman."

As we began driving back to the campsite Seton spoke in a tentative voice:

"Matt, I don't want to pry too much, but you seemed kind of offended when I asked about Lydia."

"I don't know," I said and paused a moment. "Jules liked Lydia."

"Do you feel guilty about it?"

"Well, yes."

"You shouldn't."

"Why not?"

"We all liked Jules, you know. You weren't his only friend, and you'd be crazy to think that somehow you should feel guilty about having something with Lydia. Any one of us would be happy to have something with her, and Jules would have understood too. I'm sure he would have."

I did not know how to tell him what I felt though I wanted to make some peace with him. We drove the rest of the way in silence and parked at the camp. Lydia and her friends had arrived and

112

everyone sat in chairs facing the lake as the sun set over the mountains and the shadows of the trees stretched across the water.

"Did you catch a big one?" John asked. He looked a little drunk.

"No, just a medium-sized one," I said.

Seton handed me a Busch light and we pulled up collapsible chairs.

"Shit, we're almost out of beer," John said. "I think we can get some more at Twin Lake."

"I'll go," I said and began walking up to the car.

"I'll go with you," Lydia said and walked beside me. Inside the car Lydia looked at me point blank and said:

"What the hell is going on with you?"

I put the car in drive.

"What do you mean?"

"You've been avoiding me. Perhaps I was avoiding you too, but this is getting ridiculous."

"I haven't felt well."

"Do you think I felt well? Or anyone else?"

"Well no, I didn't mean it like that."

"Well how did you mean it?"

"I don't know." I felt like a man watching the carefully woven threads of self-protection fall away as I looked on in helpless amazement. I knew the self-protection needed to fall away and I wanted to tell her everything I was feeling but my mind went blank. I didn't say anything more and Lydia sighed and looked out the window. It only took five minutes to reach the lodge of South Twin Lake on the north side of Wickiup. We walked into the cabin store and bought a couple cases of beer. After putting the beer in the car Lydia headed toward the beach. I followed her past the long stretch of white sand where a few sunbathers were packing up for the day. We walked down the dock as purple twilight settled over the small, circular lake. I remembered a day in early spring when I had jumped off that same dock into the cold water. There were still piles of snow on the banks then. Jules had sat on the edge of the dock laughing hysterically as I struggled to climb out of the water. Then I thought of another day, more recent.

"Only a month ago we stood on a dock like this one," I said.

Lydia glanced at me for a second and then started back to the car.

We drove back in a silence only heightened by the music. Back at the campsite they were trying to build a fire on the beach in a shallow pit. As we walked toward the shore I watched the silhouettes of their bodies in the light of the growing fire. They looked almost like the drunken, wild dancers I had seen painted in black on ancient Greek vases in the museums in Rome.

"Here comes the beer," John said and helped load the cooler.

We pulled up chairs around the campfire. It was now dark and the sparks from the fire burst up into the sky.

"Fuck this beer," Seton said and took a swig from a bottle of vodka. Seton handed it to me and I took a long pull from the bottle and felt the fire burn down through my throat to my gut.

"I wish Jules was here," Steven said.

The various conversations ceased with the mention of his name and a silence settled over us broken only by the cracking of the fire. John looked at me and asked,

"What was it like?"

I sat back in my chair and took another pull from the vodka. It would have to come out, I thought.

"I don't remember much. I was asleep when it happened. I had fallen asleep to music on a peaceful Sunday morning and I woke up in a car crash."

I paused for a moment and took a breath.

"When I woke the car was all smashed and the steering wheel had been driven into Jules' chest. He kept saying that he couldn't move, that he couldn't feel anything. Blood was running down my face. Then I must have fallen unconscious because the next thing I remember is the medics pulling me out of the car. I was in and out from there on. I didn't know what had happened to Jules until I woke up in the hospital."

"Jules took ecstasy the night before, didn't he?" John asked.

"Yeah. He was up all night. I came in that morning and he was sitting there listening to the music. You should have seen him that night. There was this pretty girl sitting near us on the deck and he

114

recited all of "She Walks in Beauty like the Night" to her. He kept telling her he was a poet."

My voice choked up and I stopped. After a moment I said, "I tried to write a song about him."

"Can you play it for us?" Tara asked.

I walked to the car and returned with my guitar. I removed it from the case and softly strummed a few chords. Many times I had imagined this moment, playing the song just for them. Perhaps what I had failed to say in words I could say through song.

I strummed the chords of the verse and the bright, wooden voice of the guitar grew louder. I imagined the sound of the guitar reaching into the darkness of the trees, reaching back to the place where it was born. As I sang the first line my voice cracked slightly but it only made me more determined. The melody rose in a plaintive climb and then burst into the release of the chorus. Midway through the song I looked up for a brief moment and saw the gleam of the fire in their eyes. I beat the pick hard against the strings as I entered the final chorus and then I struck the final chord and the music died away.

"That was so good. Jules would be proud," Tara said.

"Yeah, man, I can't believe you wrote that," John said.

I looked toward Lydia. Through the song she had stood a good distance from the fire and now there were tears in her eyes. She looked at me with a mixture of sadness and pride and then she turned and began walking up toward the cars.

"What the hell," John said. "I think we need to put all this behind us."

He turned on a portable stereo and the hard, manic rock music pulsed from the speakers. John began dancing around and everyone else stood up. Tara grabbed hold of my shirt and pulled me to my feet.

"Dance with me," she said.

I felt awkward dancing with her and I wondered where Lydia had gone. Finally I pulled away from Tara and joined the feverish leaping of my friends until I could hardly catch my breath and then I sprinted off into the darkness of the forest. As I walked the music grew dimmer until I heard only the occasional sound of the bass and the intermittent shouts of my friends. Through the trees I could see the scythe blade reflection of the moon on water and I walked toward the light until I came to the edge of a lagoon. I stood on the shore and looked down into the black water. It looked warm and somehow welcoming.

I thought about how easy it would be to end it there. My fingers ran over the smooth surface of the pocket knife in my hand. I slowly removed my clothes until I stood naked on the shore and the moon shone blue on my skin. A few cuts and I could walk into the water and let my life drain out of me just as Jules had felt his life drain away.

I imagined how it would feel to slip away in that black water. It would be as easy as climbing into a bath and I would leave the world in water just as I had entered it. But as I looked at the glimmering blade of the knife cool against my skin I remembered the sunrise and the river and of myself as a child looking out at the world and never imagining this day would come. I trembled then and my eyes filled with tears. I threw the pocket knife on the ground and stepped back. You crazy bastard, I thought, you've fucking lost it. I took a deep breath and laughed awkwardly to myself as people sometimes do when they feel they have escaped death. I heard a crunching to my left and I looked into the darkness of the trees. Lydia stepped slowly into the moonlight. I reached down for my clothes and stammered,

"Just a second, I've got to put my clothes on."

"Not on my account, I hope," she said and walked toward me. She put her hand on my neck and then drew herself close to me. She pulled my head down to her and kissed me. I pulled her tighter against me and the weeks of tight sorrow relaxed and drained away.

"I'm sorry," I said and wondered just how many things I was apologizing for.

"It's okay."

I put on my clothes and we walked back through the forest toward the camp. The dancing had ended with everyone either taking off into the forest or collapsing in their chairs. Lydia brought her sleeping bag over to my tent. We pulled our sleeping bags and soon we were asleep.

EPILOGUE

Later that night I woke up in the tent and quietly slipped outside. The red embers of the fire gleamed and everyone had gone to sleep. I walked down the shore on the rocky sand between the trees and the water. There was a full moon and enough light to see the knot which held the raft to the shore of the lake. I untied the rope from the trunk of a thin pine tree, climbed into the raft and pushed away from the shore. I did not know whose boat it was and could hardly care anyway. Only a fool would leave the beauty of the night to the owls.

The oars sliced the water and the boat seemed to glide over the blue haze of the lake. On the shore the dying campfires flickered like candles in cabin windows. When I had reached the center of the lake I crossed the oars over the raft and looked to the sky. The stars pulsed brightly in spite of the moon's light and I watched them with a feeling of quiet joy. A shooting star blazed across the sky and for a moment I felt as if the universe had just winked at me. I remembered as a child how I had stood on the cistern of our place in the country and danced with wild leaps as a distant thunderstorm sent electric arms reaching from the earth to the sky. I felt that way again now and I thought of how close I'd come to ending it all only a few hours before.

I felt like I had been through something. I could not say anything about it yet, but eventually I would. I remembered once when my father had shown me a cave he had found in his forest service days, a hole in the ground deep in the woods surrounded by obsidian chips. He lowered me into the mossy air of the cave and I marveled at the tall ferns that shrank in size as the darkness grew. I reached down and removed an arrowhead from a boulder and admired the precise chips that rendered the obsidian glass razor sharp. My father climbed down and lit the lantern and suddenly the walls of the cave danced with ochre drawings of the sun, animals, and strange designs.

At that moment my childhood dream of becoming an archaeologist had seemed nearer than ever. All that was gone now but what if the meaning of it endured? I would never be an archeologist but perhaps I would always be a seeker and a recorder of human experience. I could not imagine living without the meaning that dream had once given to my life, and I knew that what had stopped me at the lagoon was the idea that had once possessed my heart. I would take up Jules' story. And after that I would write others because the world needed sunlight and rivers and visions, and it needed the light and heat of childhood imagination even if it was all as fleeting as a dream.

I tied the boat back to the tree and walked along the shore to the camp. The fire was out. I climbed in the tent and into my sleeping bag. Lydia rolled over and mumbled sleepily.

"Where did you go?" she asked.

"On a journey."

"Where to?"

"Byzantium."

"Oh," she said and fell asleep again. I put my arm around her and was soon asleep.

We woke late the next morning and drove over to the lodge on South Twin Lake to eat breakfast. We sat at a long table and I looked out the window. A girl of eleven or twelve played with her younger brother. I felt very far from her and I watched her as a sailor might look back on a land to which he would never return. The young girl chased her brother across the grass and then abruptly stopped and looked self-conscious as a couple of young men walked by. It was an overcast day and the wind ruffled the lake, shook the leaves on the aspen trees and blew back the young girl's hair. Lydia leaned over to me.

"Are you happy?" she whispered.

"Yes," I said. "Right now I am."

SHORT STORIES

ISABEL

Isabel kneaded the flour in the faint blue light of the kitchen. She worked the dough slowly, two loose bangs of her chestnut hair swinging rhythmically with her motions. As she worked, she thought about how the ball of dough was smaller than an infant, pliable and sticky, but when shaped and cooked it would become a loaf with a hard crust, warm and soft inside, smelling fresh and lovely. It was strange how things like that developed, how they started small and simple and became so much more with time.

The door opened and O'Brien stood there in the fading light of day, tall and dark-haired, wearing his rough weather coat and hat. She did not look toward him as he stood there. It was enough to see him from the corner of her eye and to know why he waited like that to come in. He coughed and stepped through the doorway, his boots pounding on the loose floorboards of the house. He passed slowly in front of the kitchen table where she worked, looking at her. She stared down but saw the white of his teeth as he smiled to himself before he stepped away to stand near the warmth of the stove.

"Your mother will be here soon," he said.

She looked up at him standing with his back to her, wondering if she should say anything. He coughed again and walked around the edge of the table until he stood at her side, staring down at her. She could feel his breath on her neck, could smell the whiskey he'd drunk in the barn. She closed her eyes then and thought of the dough in her hands, of its softness, of the way it would smell when it became

120

bread. O'Brien's hands settled on her hips as he moved behind her, his body pressing gently into hers. She heard him breathe in deeply and groan almost silently, his hands moving slowly from her hips along her stomach to her breasts. They stayed there pressing firmly, and she stopped kneading the dough.

"Your mother watches you, you know? She sees you becoming a woman. She sees you replacing her, stealing her youth and beauty. Stealing her man."

She could say nothing. It was all true, even the stealing, but that he was the one stealing. His head leaned down and she felt the roughness of his beard on her neck, his hands moving down her stomach, his body pressing harder into her. She knew what would follow, how his hands would lift her skirt, how she would squeeze her eyes so tightly shut that they'd hurt, and how her nails would gouge the familiar scratches on the underside of the table.

It did not follow this time. His hands had stopped just below her stomach, waiting. Before she could think to stop herself, before she could think of why his hands had stopped or of the breath escaping her lips and forming words, she had said it:

"It is a baby."

Nothing happened. He just stood there, frozen, while her mind raced frantically to say something, anything that could change those words already spoken. At last she felt his body ease away, and heard his steps on the floorboards as he walked around the table to the stove. There he took his pipe from his coat and lit it.

"You're a foolish girl. How would you even know if you had a baby in you?" He took quick puffs from the pipe, staring out the lone window of the kitchen at the evening sky. "No, you're just a foolish little girl who wouldn't know the difference between a baby and a little belly fat. I've been too kind to you, and now you think you can get me to leave you alone with a lie." He laughed loudly. "That's it, isn't it? You little bitch." His words trailed off and Isabel looked up at last from the table.

"I haven't bled in a long time. Momma told me that's how you know when it's happened. I can feel it in there. I can feel it growing."

O'Brien began to wonder if it was true. He wished now that he'd brought the bottle of whiskey into the house. His head felt dry and unclear, and there was so much to think about.

He turned toward her, and she was afraid of the eyes that looked into hers.

"And if it was a baby, what would we do then? Kill your mother? Kill the baby?"

"You wouldn't do that. I know you wouldn't."

"And how do you know what I would or wouldn't do? Maybe it'd be easier to be rid of both of you: the old shrew and her pretty little knocked-up daughter."

She knew that he was right. And she'd seen him do so many things already, seen him beat her mother until she coughed blood, seen him shoot an Indian in the back who'd come to the farm looking for work. For all that, she did not know that O'Brien loved her, as much as such a man could love, and that he would not end the life of someone who gave him so much pleasure.

"I'm going to the barn. Finish making the bread for supper. If you say a word about this, I'll cut your Momma's throat."

Out in the yard the air was still and cold as O'Brien walked from the house to the barn. He looked in the direction of the road but could not see the silhouette of his wife's carriage returning home. She'd never before arrived home after dark, but perhaps she'd had problems with the carriage and anyway it was a moonlit night and easy for traveling.

As O'Brien entered the barn he heard the pigs rustling about in expectation of food. It felt warmer in there, perhaps from the pigs' body heat, and as he took several long sips from the jug of whiskey a feeling of comfort began to spread through him again. Of course, it was just a matter of time before his wife found out that her daughter was pregnant. But what would it matter? He knew how to deal with her, and anyway these things were not so uncommon. Hell, he'd heard that the Mormons in Salt Lake City made a virtue of it.

He thought then of Isabel, who had only been ten years old when he married her mother. At first he'd paid her no attention. It was common for women out in those parts to have children from other men, with men dying as often as they did, and it was common for new husbands to think little of it. With time though, he'd watched Isabel become a young woman, watched her body take on a shape that pleased him, even as the work of a frontier woman had worn away her mother's looks. He smiled to himself, thinking of Isabel standing there in the blue light of the kitchen, the skin of her neck so soft it made you hurt a little.

O'Brien leaned against the pig fence and took another long sip of whiskey. He felt a sudden jerk on his coat sleeve and looked down to see one of the pigs leaning its head through the fence to chew on his coat. He jerked away from the fence and slapped the pig's face,

"Nothing for you, you damn pigs."

As O'Brien raised the jug to take another sip a strange voice from the corner broke through the stillness of the barn.

"And what about us?"

O'Brien nearly choked from the shock, dropping the jug and shouting into the dark corner, "Who the hell is there? Come out and show yourself." He thought of his rifle hanging above the door of the house and wondered if he should turn and run to fetch it. "I said come out, dammit! Who the hell are you?"

The voice that replied seemed to move from one dark corner of the barn to the other, and for the first time in years O'Brien felt the ice cold grip of fear in his heart. The bodiless voice spoke clearly and distinctly in an accent that O'Brien had never heard, but which he would have guessed was European.

"We are the ones that watch. And we are the ones that give. And we are the ones that take."

O'Brien could not move. His head felt as if it was bursting out of the top of his skull. What the hell was going on? Was he losing his damn mind?

As if in reply the voice began to laugh in a high, gentle chuckle that moved around the barn, side to side, before him and even behind him. Three faint, green flames began to burn before his eyes, gradually illuminating the piles of hay in the back of the barn. O'Brien suddenly smelled something like kerosene. How could he have missed that smell all along? All at once the barn erupted in a blaze of flames that sent O'Brien reeling back out of the barn onto the cold ground of the yard. He jumped to his feet as the flames leaped out the door and the windows, racing up the sides. He had started to run to the house thinking only of the gun above the door when he froze in his tracks.

On the road that ran along the ridge above the house a ball of fire was moving. At first, that was all O'Brien could make of it, but as it drew closer down the road he began to guess what it might be, although he could not allow himself to imagine that it was true. The neighing of the horses finally gave it away, a shrieking animal scream that grew louder and louder until the horses stormed into the yard drawing the blazing carriage behind them. O'Brien could do nothing but back away towards the house as they passed through the yard and away, the flames racing down the harnesses and engulfing the horses, the charred, faceless body of his wife bouncing up and down on the carriage seat.

At last O'Brien turned and ran the last steps to the door of the house, thinking of the gun, thinking of murder and revenge. He ran in so quickly that he did not notice Isabel standing there, not until he had reached up to find a bare wall above the door and glanced desperately around the room for the gun. Only then did he see Isabel's profile in the darkness still standing there at the kitchen table. He stepped slowly toward her, whispering her name a few times. She stood there as she always did in the evenings, with her head turned down at the dough in her hands. Only now there was a knife in her belly, and a thin rope tied round her neck from the ceiling held her upright.

O'Brien knew that she was gone, but instinctively he walked around behind her and put his hands on her hips, and leaned his head down to rest his lips on her cold neck. How long he stayed there he could not be certain. Seconds or minutes or hours, there was nothing but a cold emptiness in him that stretched on as far as he could feel. Eventually he walked away though, taking short, involuntary strides through the room and into the yard still bright with the flames of the barn. When something cold and heavy against his neck brought him down to the ground, O'Brien could barely manage to roll on his back to defend himself. If he'd known what awaited him perhaps he would not have turned over at all.

At first, he could not tell if it was a man or an animal. His eyes were blurred and all he could make out was a massive head like that of a bear, with horns on either side, moving towards him with quick, jerking motions against a backdrop of fire. As it reached O'Brien the creature reeled up tall, a silver blade flashing over its head, before falling forward and plunging the knife into O'Brien's stomach.

O'Brien shouted in agony as he felt the knife in his body, cutting through his spine and leaving everything below numb. He tried to move but felt the creature pin down his arms, straddling his body with its legs. A voice began to speak in a language he did not understand, and he struggled to open his eyes against the pain. Slowly, through tears and screams, he began to make out the shape of a man's face beneath the bear's head, an old man's face surrounded by long white hair, eyes closed and lips moving as he spoke unknown words.

The man reached behind him and jerked the knife out of O'Brien's stomach, provoking a fresh onslaught of screams. O'Brien felt a large, strong hand wrap around his head and grasp his hair. He felt the knife begin to cut through the skin of his upper forehead, felt the hair and skin of his scalp begin to pull away. He began to feel far away, hearing the screams of another man, and he knew he was going to die. The old man's words continued as O'Brien began to fall into the darkness, the last image passing through his mind of Isabel kneading the flour in the faint blue light of the kitchen.

THE CURSE OF SPROUT

What is Sprout doing, in her hut by the sea, her rotted-out van become a home? Far from the madding likes of the village, yet still within sight. Still within sight of me in my mountain crypt. I am the poor girl's father-lover. Why do I always look to love to save me? As if the love of some young girl could undo what the centuries have done to me. Yet I am fair to look upon, caught forever in the last bloom of my youth. I was thirty-seven when they made me. My last hair had just turned grey, yet I was still youthful and virile. To outward appearances I remain so.

Under all these layers what is there to tell? The girl that came to enchant me so, long after I had ceased believing myself even capable of it. She woke me from my deep sleep. I don't know how many years had passed in that near deathless hibernation. And when I woke the world had changed. Some epidemic had struck humankind and they were now scarce and no longer lived in cities. The small village near Sprout's hut was the only human habitation I had come across in my nocturnal wanderings. And it was hardly even a village. More like some caravan of vehicles that had run out of fuel and turned into a stable home.

It was in my hibernation that she came to me. Always the explorer, she found a way into my cave and I woke to the sight of her green eyes paralyzed by fear as well as curiosity. I could feel my hunger and so I took her. For three days I kept her in my cave, feeding on her, fucking her, giving her orgasms the likes of which she'll never know again. I see her pale, perfect body on my bed, her ass arched upward as I fuck her from behind, draining her blood and planting my lifeless seed. It is all too much to bear. She has left me now, for some wanderer and the open road. Yet here I am, left behind to rot in my cave, to dream and desire. Will I stay awake when consciousness has become such agony? Or will I return to the sleep of centuries to wake and find humanity extinct? Marxentius am I. The shadow man.

Last night I went down to the village and walked among their filthy huts and dry-rot vehicles. I found nothing to my desire so I went into the mountains and drank from a young doe. All animals come to me when I desire. They lay down before me so I can taste for a moment the remembrances of a life that was stolen from me.

I was just a boy when I first met one like me, one of the undying. He too lived in a cave, in that land I once called my home, the dry deserts of Oregon. Like Sprout, I had also been an explorer. There were many lava tubes on the properties surrounding our country home. I made it my business to explore each of them. I found him at the back of a long cave, a still body draped in black, filthy, bearded, and I took him for a corpse. I reached out a finger to touch his neck, yet his eyes opened and he smiled at me.

"Welcome to eternity," he said, and the world went black. I awoke at the mouth of the cave, exhausted and nearly lifeless. It took me years to understand what I had met in that cave that I afterwards avoided.

They say that our kind was formed in the smithy of the world's fire, in the furnace blast that made all life. We are life as well, after all. Even our hearts beat, yet so slowly that only a single beat may happen in the span of a human's life. That is the secret of our longevity.

Yet I grow sick of writing about me. I am consumed by thirst, for Sprout's intoxicating blood. This mere girl who captivated an immortal. The thirst never leaves me but in the deepest, most silent clutches of my deathsleep. Where is she now? Let me find her in my thoughts.

Sprout awoke to the wet leaves of the morning dew, the air cool and still in the forest where she camped. She listened to Grosvenor's snores as he slept beside her on the tattered green tarp. The sky was lightening, pink in the direction the sun would rise. She reached out to touch Grosvenor's dick through his pants. She could feel the outline of it, stiff with the morning. She undid his zipper and pulled it out, stroking it into more ardent life. Grosvenor's snores ended. He arched his back and yawned, enjoying this morning ritual. It was always fun to travel with Sprout.

I feel myself plucked out of the vision by the agony of this realization: it was once my dick she liked to fondle in the morning. It was me sleeping beside her. After those first three days with her I let her leave, doubting she would ever return. Yet she did return, one month later in the darkness of the new moon, that time when my powers are at their greatest.

She shouted from the mouth of the cave, "Marxentius!?"

There was a playful lightness in her voice, as if she was making a joke. I wondered for a moment if it was a trap, if hordes of villagers waited outside the cave with pitchforks ready to fill me with holes. My kind are not used to warm receptions from those who know what we are. Still, I decided to come to her voice. I rose from the dark corner where I had been resting in a reverie. I spend most of my time doing that. When you have lived for many centuries the past becomes a world more enticing than the present. The peaks and valleys of life come to be more real than the level plains of the unfolding present.

But here was a peak of interest, this sexy young girl who called out my name in a playful manner like it was all a joke. I found her leaning against the oak tree that hid the entry to my cave.

"Hello," I said.

"Hey! Do you want to go on an adventure with me?"

We walked through the forest in silence until we came to a cliff overlooking the sea. Silence is my most familiar companion. My words are few except when I'm freshly fed and relaxed. I had already tasted blood that day yet the first pangs of new desire would soon be upon me.

It was pleasurable to walk through those woods on a dark night, the stars especially bright through the gaps in the forest canopy. The leaves rustled in the softest movements of air from the sea. She only broke the silence once, when my long strides had carried me ahead of her.

"Can you not walk so far ahead of me?"

And so I slowed my purposeful pace to match her leisurely stride, walking alongside her. I almost wondered if I should hold her hand, though the idea seemed absurd. And there was something about Sprout that told me she disliked the romantic, that to her mind such gestures were meaningless, or a sign of weakness.

At the seaside cliffs we sat down on a pair of boulders and looked down at the sea and the distant light of the village.

"Will you promise me something?" she asked.

"If I can."

"That you will never tell anybody else about what we did in the cave. Or about anything else we are going to do?"

"I promise," I said, thinking little of it but that it was a strange request. My life was not exactly blooming with friends and social engagements. And why would I tell anyone about this girl, who at that time was just a girl I had fucked and feasted on?

"Good," she said, and stood up. She pulled off her shirt and dropped her skirt. She stood there naked to me in the inky blue light, and I felt my desire return like a hammer to the chest.

"I want you to do it to me again, from behind. Lay me down on that boulder and fuck me again."

As commanded I laid her against the boulder and put my cock in her warm cunt. It felt warmer this time. Wetter, and as she undulated between the boulder and my body I felt a softness come over me. Not over my cock. That thing was rigid and at purpose, yet there was a softness in my heart, a rush of warm feeling for the girl. I bit down into the soft flesh between her neck and shoulder. I came in her as I drank her blood and started to wonder, "do I love this girl?" My deepest sin is that I am most turned on sexually by the thought of love, of love in its deepest, most anatomical truth, the merging of two fleshly bodies to create a new one. Could she give life to my deathless seed? Could she be a vessel for this life?

Afterward we lay beside each other on the boulder as I admired her nakedness, her ripe, full breasts, her hot cunt dripping with my dark seed.

"It's strange how I feel when you cum inside me. It's like I can feel you inside me even when you are no longer there."

I lay back thinking about this.

"Hey, come hang out, it's cold," she said.

I laughed at the expression. "Come hang out" as a way of asking to cuddle. I held her close. Again this sensation of love, almost unfamiliar and new after so long alone.

"So what turns you on?" she asked.

"This," I said, my finger reaching to fill the small dimple above her immaculate ass. She giggled and said that it tickled her.

I feel pulled away from that sweet memory to a time long ago, when I was still a human, to a grand old house on St. Charles Avenue in New Orleans. It was a house I had all to myself at the ripe age of twenty-four. All my life I have known the vastness of solitude and the expansion of self in that space. At twenty-four I was an orphan, my parents killed in a traffic accident and nobody to call family. At first, I was devastated. After all the details had been put to rest and I came to take up residence in the family home, I admitted to myself moments of delight in my solitude. Ever since I was a child in the country I've felt this tingling in my balls at moments of departure. When I am left alone, I exult. Yet I am also the loneliest creature I have ever known.

I recall one evening at that house in New Orleans. We called it Dolly's house after my great-grandmother who had lived nearly all her life in it. We were sitting by the pool in the backyard on a warm night in May. My new artist friend, Aaron, and I sat sat at the pool's edge, drinking our wine. Two girls swam in the pool, Aaron's friends who I had just met. One of the girls had green eyes and the full-figured feminine body that I adore. We kept making eye contact as the girls swam in circles, holding the gazes longer than necessary. She was to become my first great love, Amara, who I loved like the sea.

I welcomed her into the darkness of my world, and even then it was dark. We became traveling companions, living in Italy and Greece while working on organic farms. Eventually we came to despise each other yet neither of us had the strength to let it go. At last we decided on a separation that became absolute once she'd found a new lover.

Thus began my habit of being the one left behind, even when it could said that my misery manipulatively drives them away emotionally before they choose to actually depart. What am I talking about though? I'm growing bored of my own story. So let me tell another.

Sprout was born after the great epidemic. Her parents were scrappers and tinkerers, wandering the great wastes of the world from camp to camp, trading and fixing things. When she came of age her father began to have sex with her and her mother became increasingly jealous of her daughter. The situation became uncomfortable for her and so she ran off with a tinkerer she met in a camp. She had been wandering ever since. That is the story of her survival, her sex, and her strength. I came to love all of it.

After that night at the cliff she came to see me more regularly, and some nights I visited her in her tire-less van shelter. We'd tussle and then lie awake talking, the stars shining through the sunroof of the van. She liked to hear my stories, of all the places I had been and the people I had loved. She wanted to know what sex had been like with other women. It turned her on.

Some nights I came to see her even when I knew she wasn't there. I wanted to imagine that maybe it was different than it was, that Sprout didn't take off on a whim sometimes with other men. It made me sad that she did so. She was my only companion and the only thing that kept me from drifting again into the deathsleep.

I couldn't stop her from doing what she wanted to do, didn't want to stop her. I wanted to fill her with my love, and when I was honest with myself her promiscuity turned me on.

And so it went on like this for some months. When Sprout was around we fucked and we feasted. When she wasn't I sulked in my cave feeding my thirst on animals, trying to appease a slakeless desire. In some way that is how I came to love only one woman, though at times in my life I had been a rake and loved many. I call it Sprout's Curse.

In the beginning all things thrive and shine with usefulness. Even love is this way. It is constantly changing, constantly dying and being reborn. It seeks the sea, and the channels are ever-changing.

When did things start to change with Sprout? How did we go from simple sexual communion to bitter animosity? That first time she ran away, after our first few months together. I realized I missed her. I loved her. I didn't really want anybody other than her. It took her departure for me to realize this, and whenever I have experienced the moment of realizing I'm in love I simultaneously become aware of its shadow side. With the onset of attachment comes the fear of loss. The greater the desire the stronger its inverted expression as fear. Would she still let me have her when she returned, I wondered? When she did return I found her alone in her van, tinkering by candlelight with some new gadgets she had acquired. She seemed unsurprised by my arrival, neutral in her diffidence. I told her of my feelings for her. Then she seemed a little surprised and caught off guard. I asked her why she'd left me to wander with another.

"Don't you remember, the night before I left?"

I struggled for a moment to remember. We had been spending every night together for about a week. I was lying in my cave, drunk and gluttonous on her blood and her sex. She wanted me to come with her to the village that night for the feast. I said I didn't want to. I was tired and had already over-feasted. Besides, they would see what I am and reject me. She said they would not see my nature. She kept pushing and I gave in. We walked down to the village where the bonfire burned bright, and the villagers danced, and drank, and feasted. They were dirty and unclean, crude and directionless, these children of humanity's fall. I was awkward and withdrawn, often wandering out of the camp light to sit in silence by myself, resting in my reveries until she'd come to find me and urge me to come back and dance and play music. She'd lean over so I could see the ample swell of her breasts, coaxing me back into desire. The villagers paid me little mind, lost in their ecstasy, though they gathered around when I picked up a guitar and began to play the songs of another age. They were transfixed by these stories of the old world. I soon grew tired though and set the guitar aside. I had been a musician once and my blood drunken clumsiness as I played agitated me. The songs brought to life a world that no longer existed, a world I grieved in its passing.

As the night grew late I noticed a wanderer speaking often to Sprout. She said he was her friend. I grew irritable and told Sprout I wanted to rest. We spent the night in her van and in the morning she straddled me and said she had to go do work in the village. I thought little of it and went back to my cave.

That night her van shelter was empty, and remained so for some nights to come. Now, sitting with her, I asked her what that night had meant to her.

"You were such an asshole to everyone, especially to Dreyfus who was just my friend. You acted like a jealous asshole."

"Is Dreyfus the one you left with?"

"Yes."

"And does he have feelings for you?"

"Obviously."

"Then why wouldn't I be jealous?"

"Don't you see that it pushed me away though? You're always saying how we come from different worlds, anyway. I didn't see it until that night. You couldn't just hang and have a good time."

"Why would I want to hang with them?"

"Because that's what you do with people. Or maybe you don't. Maybe you just sulk in your cave all the time. Anyway, I don't really want to sit around talking about this all night. I need to work."

I wandered away from her back into the night, the erotic dispelled by the mundane, the arrows of her words too sharp to defend myself against. So began my slow return to human form, a long and painful process driven by my love for Sprout. There used to be a place in City Park in New Orleans, a bayou with many oak trees heavy with spanish moss. A stone bridge crossed a thin waterway and led to a tiny island. Across the bayou there stood a Greek Revival Peristyle with ionian columns and guarded by two lion statues. I used to go there to write and play music. Of all the places in New Orleans that was where I felt closest to the natural breathing heart of that strange and ancient place. I felt alive there, close to nature yet surrounded by a city.

What sounds can we make at the edge of tomorrow and today? What species of interest can we speak to carry the anger away? Asleep and in dreams I am with her. Always there is something dark about it. The bruises I left on her body. In my dreams they are there although I never struck her in real life, only with my words and the agony of my heart. Maybe I never wanted it. Maybe I could feel her starting to fall for me and so I sabotaged it, despite all the pain I would suffer for my decisions. That Bayou Metairie in City Park that calls to me — the ancient portages and pathways of that space.

I never knew quite what to say to her, this girl that confounded me so. I hear her high voice singing sweetly while she tinkered. I wanted to go on hearing that voice, but I destroyed it all in the end. Drove her away from me. I did not listen to all that was underneath her words. In the end it was my fault because I was her elder by centuries and I was the main man in her life. I was the one she asked things of, and I did not deliver. What to say of it all now?

What did I expect would happen? That she could somehow be happy with me? That she could be content with my cave life, or I with her wanderer's life? In the end though, I became the wanderer, without her at my side. I feel called into the world again, to share the lost songs and stories with the children of humanity. My heart begins to beat again in rhythm with the pace of life.

TO FISH, TO DRINK, AND TO LIVE

The river flowed past me like a shooting star in the night sky and to be there watching it flow made more sense than anything that had occurred in the last few weeks. It was like a shooting star in that I could see its true nature for only a second, and then it was gone. The memory of having understood the river stayed in my mind, but it was like the memory of a dream, vague and unclear. After that it was just water flowing over basalt rock bottom working its way to larger rivers and finally to the sea. It felt good to be there watching the pure, blue water flow over shallow boulders and rocks, but I had not come to watch the water flow, I came to fish.

I cast a silver spinner out into the current and slowly reeled it in, watching as it slipped past rocks and boulders, probing into every hole where a fish could be waiting. I fished there but caught nothing, so I walked farther down until I came to a bridge that crossed the river. Under the bridge there was a dark blue hole, and on the bottom were a few black shapes, pointing upstream like torpedoes. I cast into the hole and reeled in, waiting, excitement building, every muscle in my body wanting to pull back and set the hook into a huge trout. I saw a shadow dash out from the darkness of the hole, I set the hook, and there was the trout. The trout struggled into the current, and I knew he was a big one. He fought like mad thrashing his head back and forth, stealing line from my reel and making the tip of my rod shake and dance. I fought the trout until he tired, then I brought him in, heavy and slowly and then he was there next to the bank. I reached down into the cold water and touched the fish, cradling him and feeling his great size and thickness. His sides were a golden brown with black spots all along his back. His teeth were small and sharp, a voracious tiger of the stream. The fish was heavy and slimy and good to hold all at the same time. When I finally released the fish back into the current it was like saying goodbye to a friend. I walked up the steep embankment and down the road to the camp.

The dirt road went parallel to the river and between the road and the river there were campsites nestled in pine trees. On the other side of the road was a grass airstrip, and all along the airstrip small Cessna planes were lined up. I walked a while down the road looking at the planes but not really thinking about them. The fishing had cleared my mind the way only fishing can. A good day of fishing is like the first real day of spring, when the sun shines brilliantly from blue skies and the warm air drives away the pensive greyness of winter's interminable days.

When I reached camp I saw that everyone was hitting the booze pretty hard. Murray came up to me and put a whiskey-coke in my hand.

"Did you catch anything?" Murray asked me. He was in high spirits.

"Yeah, I caught a big brown," I said.

"Really, you like fishing?"

"Yeah."

"I'll take you out on Crane Prairie some time. We'll kill some big bastards."

Murray was a big guy who loved life. I knew that he loved life and that was what drew people to him, despite what a jerk he could be at times. Murray had a mustache and reddish blond hair. He could not talk more than five seconds without using some swear word. It was easy to imagine him as a bear, looking for honey and mad as hell if he didn't get it.

I took a sip from the whiskey-coke and felt it go down to my stomach, where it stoked a nice little fire. I sat on a log facing the fire. The light of day was slowly dying and the Idaho sky was turning dark. The darkness came like a blanket over the land, bringing a still peace to everything. Sparks erupted into the night sky, every little spark a fleck of warmth and light. Sitting there it all made sense. I was here now and that was all that mattered. I could not imagine not having the world in front of me, and all I wanted to do was live. To live each day as if death was visiting me the next, and to live life with no regrets. The gates to my mind opened then and a surge of ideas and thoughts flowed out. The night went by and soon was over, passing as easily as the water in the river that flowed nearby.

I woke with a great thirst. My mouth was a desert that had once known rain. I drank water out of a canteen. The morning had come and a cool breeze was carrying the scent of early morning to my nose. The early morning smell is something I will always have. It is the smell of all things new and fresh and of unlimited opportunities. It rises up from the soil and trees, bringing a fresh day with it like the first glint of sunrise. I dressed in a daze, my head pounding but my body ready to go. I walked to the plane shining in the sun. The metal of the plane was warm to touch. The plane sat there like a great metal bird, aching to be free, up in the sky without a care. Murray and I climbed into his plane. The engine sputtered and came to life. We taxied out onto the grass and slowly sped up. The grass and the trees became a blur of green and then we lifted off, and we were flying. The plane rose up out of the canyon. At the bottom of the canyon I could see the river and the grass airstrip, and at the end of the airstrip there was a yellow house. I saw how the river flowed through the canyon, past the hard, gray cliffs like a serpent through grass and stones. The plane flew up out of the canyon and then above huge monolithic mountains, rising hard and jagged into the sky. They stood there hard and permanent, unchanging like the sun. Ahead of us a green plain of grasses and hills and rivers touched a sky of golden clouds and infinite light. It was like a hundred days, a hundred different experiences compressed into one moment, and it was beautiful and it was simple. I watched it all spread before me like an impossible dream and I could not see past the moment, I could enjoy only what was there before me and the life I had to live.

THE GOD OF THE ISLAND

He dreamed of a desolate, wild valley in the red-orange light just after sunset. A tall and thin tower rose from the middle of the valley. A huge black creature soared in wide arcs around it. Moving closer he saw the dragon prepare to land on the tower's pinnacle, and he could make out the shape of a man riding the dragon to its landing, its huge wings beating as its legs extended and grasped the roof of the tower. The dragon's neck elongated and from its mouth blew fire down into the valley. A column of fire reached down from the height of the tower to rake the ground, the dead, blackened branches immersed in flame. The dragon breathed fire in a wide arc and then stopped as the man, dressed in dark robes with with white hair, stepped down off the dragon and disappeared down a flight of stairs

In a cave-like chamber the wizard emerged from a staircase. He walked to a podium in the center of the room with an oddly shaped object upon it. He faced it and raised his hands as the object began to glow, brightening into a black obsidian stone with a large flat surface full of images - of people and places bright and full of life in contrast to the fire-scorched land and dark tower. The face of the old man could be seen just behind the stone, his features illuminated by it and looking fierce and intent, suddenly changing to tenderness followed by a soft wave of his hand. The images on the stone coalesced into a scene with a boy sitting with another wizard in an idyllic forest setting, a pool of clear water behind them. The wizard winced from some pain and the boy said,

138

"Master, is it not possible for you to change yourself back to a boy, like myself, and to live life over again?"

The old man smiled a little. "That is a power denied to all mortals, even to the strongest and wisest. Only the gods have such powers."

The scene shifted to a bedroom where the old wizard lay visibly dead in the bed, a handsome young man kneeling at the edge of the bed sobbing. The eyes of the wizard now in the chamber of the great tower became moist, his face full of grief. Swiftly he raised his arms and channeled some energy into the stone which glowed red hot. A whirlwind began to swirl around the wizard and the stone, growing in color and speed until the man's face subtly transformed into that of the handsome young man again. The storm subsided and the room was still. The stone had become a mirror. The young face smiled and then started to fade away. The wizard's youthful face, now hazy and incorporeal, drifted away revealing again the old man. The black stone absorbed the youthful face, emitting a surge of glowing light as the face disappeared. The old man stood hunched and defeated, sorrow heavy in his face.

Suddenly a frightful rage replaced his sadness. The wizard stood tall and shot jets of electricity from his hands down into the rock floor of the tower. Outside, shockwaves rolled away from the bass of the tower. The dragon, wakened from sleep, took to wing. The wizard channeled the energy downward until all at once he stopped, in a moment of absolute silence appearing to grow small and frail. Outside the shockwaves and tendrils of electricity flowed back from the valley and into the tower. The chamber began to shake and explode with light, the energy suffusing his body. His arms reached out and began to guide the energy, and slowly he was transformed into a hideous winged creature. His eyes glowed red and his body was deformed and frail. He ran out of a passage and out of a hollow of the tower taking flight across the valley.

He flew with long languid beats of his wings leaving the valley behind, passing over snowy mountains and then gliding down to a sleepy little village. He landed silently on a balcony, walking to a small framed window. Inside a young woman was sleeping. Her brow tightened, as if from a bad dream. The wizard held up his palm and with the other hand conjured a ghostly halo of scenes of forests and peaceful animals. He blew the halo softly and it passed through glass, floating across the room and disappearing against the forehead of the sleeping girl. Her face became serene again as a black misshapen mass poured through the window gathering form again at the foot of the bed. The wizard raised his palm again and conjured another halo, this time with images of a handsome young man. The girl arched her back a little and sighed. The wizard pulled the blanket off the bed revealing her naked body. He covered her and began to make love, the old man vaguely visible beneath the monster. She remained sleeping but actively responsive to his movements. At the moment of trembling climax his mouth opened with fangs bared. He bit down into her neck and drained away her blood.

The sleeping girl lay pale and dead as the wizard soared out over the rooftops, his flight more steady and powerful. Down a dark road a young man walked. Hearing a sound he stopped and peered into the darkness around him. The wizard bore down on him from above, drinking from the man until his body fell aside lifeless. The wizard thrust his gaze upward as his body became fuller, his musculature distinct. He flew swiftly into the sky, flying high above the land and the clouds and gliding in the moonlight and starlight. He dropped into a long dive plunging into the sea aways from the rocky shore. Down into the dark water his body shot with wings clasped tightly around him, slowing as he reached the dim outlines of the seafloor where he came to rest. A wave of his hand caused phosphorescent light to illuminate the rocky bottom of the sea where many bright fish swam around. With one of his long claws he cut his wrist and the blood flowed strongly into the black depths. He waited with head lowered. A massive shark swam lazily out of the blackness, its jaws opened to swallow the wizard. At the last moment the wizard's hands grasped the shark's jaws, struggled a moment, and then tore the lower jaw away. The shark reeled on its side as the wizard's claws ripped into the animal, removing its heart and drinking from it as the great body of the shark drifted along the seafloor.

Out of the surface of the nighttime sea the wizard exploded into the air, winging swiftly across the sea as the first rays of dawn began to shine. He pulled up short in his flight, hovering a moment as a small island began to take shape before him, and then flew down toward the lush tropical island and into a sea cave. The cave was richly adorned with bright shells and stones, a channel of shining emerald water cutting through the center. A loom sat in one corner with strands of bright gold thread hanging. The wizard stared at it for a moment and then looked down into the water.

"Calypso?" he said in a deep resounding voice which echoed supernaturally through the cavern, as if taken up and sung by watery choirs.

The water began to take human shape and stepping onto the solid ground of the cave became a beautiful goddess.

"Odysseus?" she asked tremblingly as she looked at his repugnant form. "Why have you come to me after so long away, and in so repellent a form? Do not think I have forgotten the handsome man who washed up here many years ago."

"You see me as I am: crippled and deformed by old age yet still possessing the strength of many years."

She looked at him with compassion and with a wave of her hand the monster transformed into the old man, naked and vulnerable. She walked to him and took him in her arms.

"And why have you come to see me, Odysseus?"

"For a purpose I had not known until this moment."

He grasped her lustrous body and they fell to the sandy floor of the cave as he kissed and caressed her body.

"I see now that for all your appearance may say about you, your strength has grown well beyond that of a man. To what purpose do you gather it so deliberately?"

"For this," he said as his face became contorted and fangs appeared, biting into the neck of the goddess. Her head rolled back as he drank the silver blood that leaked from his mouth. Throughout the surrounding sea the relentless procreative urge gave way suddenly to mass death, the essence of life flowing into the body of the goddess as the wizard drained her. Her death scream filled the cave and was taken up by the sea surrounding the island, the waves growing wild. The goddess fell away from his grasp, her body turning to liquid that flowed away into the channel, the echoing screams fading to silence. The wizard rose up now a young man again with eyes glowing green like the sea, hair dreaded and aquatic.

He smiled darkly with his pride, stepping forward swiftly on to the water as if to tread across its surface. But then he halted, staring down as his leg became translucent and watery. The translucence spread up his back leg and he started to sink into the sea. Desperately he stepped back onto land and watched as the translucence sank away. He stared in confusion at the water. The voice of the goddess echoed in the cavern as the walls shimmered with her words.

"You are become the God of the Island. To the sea you owe your unchanging youthful form, and to the sea you are now bound, forever the servant of that god you have always despised: lordly, mysterious Poseidon.

Anguish fell across the wizard's face as he understood, and Cody felt himself being pulled backward out of the cave, pulled backward away from the island now beautiful in the dawn's light rising over the sea's horizon.

VALHALLA, OR THE VIKING'S PARADE

Of late, Craig had taken to wearing the black cowboy boots and silver belt buckle of his wife's dead father. His wife and child took silent notice of the change. The new clothes complemented what he considered a wonderful new time in his life. The secrecy of his affair also lent a certain dangerous excitement to an otherwise dreary life. He could remember, with the feverish nostalgia of the love-struck male, the slow progression of the affair from the commonplace flirting of the office to full-fledged adultery. In retrospect it was hard to point out one moment that marked the shift, and he rather liked to think of himself as a naïve victim of love. The day it happened they were eating lunch at his favorite Thai restaurant, and they were both feeling the effects of the drinks consumed over the course of the meal.Perhaps the moment she made the offer in the restaurant marked the movement of their relationship from coquetry to adultery. She had put it innocently enough:

"Do you want to come have a drink at my place before we go back to work?"

In the back of his mind Craig should have fully realized what she was asking of him. But beneath the haze of the immediate moment, amplified all the more in its intensity by the drinks, the repercussions of this act remained inconspicuous. It all seemed so right at the time, how she put on Peter Frampton at her house and handed him a shot of tequila. The music sent him back to a warm spring day on the college campus of his youth, the bikinied girls stretched out in the sun

143

across the grassy quad, the pungent smell of weed in the air, and the music of Peter Frampton playing. It was natural the way she pulled up into his arms after taking the shot of tequila, the flowery smell of her blond hair, the fullness of her body beside his. And then they lunged at each other with the desperate intensity of long-concealed desires finally realized. Her naked body, tanned and voluptuous, was so different from the pale skin of his dark-haired wife. They made love with his hands gripping her ass, her tits hanging in his face. When it was over they smoked some pot, lying next to each as the smoke curled up and caught in the beams of afternoon light coming through the window shutters.

Craig drove past the snow-sprinkled fields thinking about what he had to do. At the office party the night before he had had too much to drink. His wife had sat at the corner table watching him dance with the secretary, watching how they laughed and stared into each other's eyes. She watched and all the while something in her slowly gave way and broke like ice in the spring.

Now Craig would have to tell his son that his parents were separating. He parked his car beside the end of the runway of the small rural airport. He needed to prepare himself, he thought as he looked out at the fading blue winter sky and the purple hills to the east.

He could tell Brian was in a good mood when he picked him up at his brother's house. The ten-year old boy always enjoyed spending the night at his cousin's house. The boy's appreciation for playmates was all the more acute owing to the relative isolation of his own home on ten acres out in the country.

As they drove down the road Brian noticed that his father's eyes were misty. This was an uncommon event indeed, since the only time Brian could remember seeing his father cry was after watching *Dances with Wolves*.

"Dad, what's wrong?"

"Your mother wants us to separate for awhile."

II

I suppose you could say I'm a typical kid. I have my obsessions, my fantasies. I'm going to become a famous archaeologist like Indiana Jones. I have already started my research into the lost city of Atlantis, which someday I plan on unearthing to the world. I read a lot, and I love to play outside. We have a rope tied to the tree in our front yard, and I can spend hours swinging around on it, imagining that I'm escaping a booby-trapped temple or defeating a gang of no-good thieves on a ship in the ocean. There is also a big cistern in our front yard, and I like to pretend it's a castle. I spend most of my time running around imagining things, like I'm a Viking and the crumbling rock wall on our property is really a great battlement. Sometimes I go to my cousin's house. He lives just down the street past the airport. At his house there is a big pond we play in during the summer, and our Grandma always calls to say we need to wear sun block, SPF 25, or we'll get cancer. We never wear sun block.

On the day my father came to pick to me up we had been riding motorcycles around their property for hours, so I was in a great mood. And then I saw his tears and he told me what was happening. I had never imagined that something like this could happen. Only troubled families had divorces.

Of course, I should have known something was going on. For months my father seemed a different person, far from the quiet man I remember chopping wood with in the fall. I remember one day we worked for hours chopping wood and stacking it, and you could smell winter on the cold wind. He did not say much as we worked, only that I needed to have more motivation. But then when we went inside the house he made me a bowl of clam chowder. I sat close to the blue wood stove with the glass door, so that you could see the roaring blaze inside like the flames of hell. It was all warm in the house and it felt so good after the cold. And then I saw that Young Indiana Jones was on TV and we sat together and watched it, my father and I.

My father had become quite a bit different since then. Now he always tucked his shirts into his jeans, and listened to old rock like the Allman Brothers in his car, and some other guy who I like because he sings about fireflies and stars and getting away from the city. I feel like he does.

I had also noticed the way he talked to that secretary at his office, the one with the raspy voice who I did not like. When they talked to each other it seemed a lot like flirting, which I'd heard about at school.

III

Craig and his wife and son decided to take a drive together on the Sunday after the day they decided they were going to separate. Craig's wife, Stacie, sat in the passenger side of the Isuzu Trooper as they drove out into the high desert hills east of town. She tried not to look at Craig, feeling that the very sight of him would be enough to rouse her wrath, and she didn't want to do that in front of her son. Craig was silent as well, concentrating on the road and his thoughts. The only sound in the car came from Brian.

"Mom, why do you want to separate? Dad doesn't want to. Only bad families get divorces. Remember in the Bible how you showed me that it is wrong to get a divorce. What about the Bible, Mom?"

"Brian, it is not my choice. What your father did…"

"Can't you guys just work on it?"

Brian felt the tears coming back and that awful welling in his chest like a dam about to burst. He waited for an answer. His father was silent as they drove on down the highway. They turned off onto a dirt road that led to Pine Mountain, a rather undistinguished butte in the middle of dry sage desert with an observatory on top.

"Dad, pull over, I want to walk in the snow."

They stopped the car and Brian ran out into the snow which was crusted over and broke beneath every step. His mother watched him stomping through the snow in his fedora hat and the blue coat they had bought him for Christmas. She remembered with a laugh how only months ago she had noticed body odor on her child, and had bought him his first stick of deodorant. She thought then of the tall

146

blond man she had met the night before at the bar. Craig had not even noticed him, busy as he was with that skanky secretary. The man had looked at her intently with his blue eyes, introducing himself in his strange but appealing Norwegian accent.

THE TOWER OF MONTE CIRCEO

On a spring day in Italy two men and one woman followed a path around Monte Circeo away from the long stretch of white sand called Sabaudia. The mountain was the mythical home of Circe, the temptress who turned men into animals, until Odysseus arrived and foiled her plans. It juts into the sea midway between Rome and Naples and there is an ancient rock tower that once served as a lighthouse midway up the mountain. The two students and the woman had driven out from Rome that morning after a night of drinking. The path they followed ended abruptly and below them the emerald water stretched into the depths of a sea cave.

The men were dark-haired and could have passed for Italians, but they were Americans studying in Italy for the spring semester. The taller one was standing on the edge of the drop-off looking down into the water. The shorter stocky one, Mike, was speaking softly to the woman, Dania, an Italian in her mid-twenties who had studied at the American university in Rome.

"Are you going to jump in Matteo?" Mike asked with a grin as he watched his roommate.

Matt was kneeling down looking into the water and thinking about how he would find his way out of the water once he jumped in. He knew it would be cold, but nothing could be as cold as the lake he jumped into in March when he was sixteen, when the snow was piled up along the banks.

"Yeah, I just don't know how I'm going to get out once I jump in," Matt said.

But finally he stood and stepped back a few paces and then ran

148

forward launching himself off the ledge. He felt a sudden panic in his gut as the green water rushed up at him and an ancient instinct kicked in making him shout, making the fall seem to last forever until he plunged through the surface. A powerful shiver passed through his body as he struggled up towards the surface, to the light, and then he broke through the surface and breathed deeply. As he swam beside the rocks he felt the ache of cold burning through him until it subsided into numbness. He found a boulder with a few handholds and soon he was out of the water and sitting on a black rock hot from the sun.

"Looks kind of cold," said Mike with a laugh.

Mike decided to head to the tower and Matt watched as he rounded the mountain. Dania sat down beside him.

"Do you remember what I was saying last night, about you staying this summer?" she asked. "We could come here every week and make love in this place. Would you like that?"

Her voice was soft but awkwardly inflected with a British accent she had picked up when she studied in London. He smiled but kept his eyes out on the sea. He felt a little too cold to start up that conversation. Then she moved closer and he felt the sudden warmth of her body and the fragrance of her hair and skin washed over him and he leaned over to kiss her. She asked if he wanted to go to the tower but he felt like staying there for a little longer.

After she left, he stood and began climbing straight up the mountain side until he found a small ledge and could look out at the stretch of beach and down at the rocks where the swirling water rushed in white and submerged the rocks. It was beautiful the way the sunburnt skies stretched above him and down to where the sea met the sky. He looked up at the mountain and listened to the sweet rushing of the waves on the rocks below. Slowly but powerfully he felt a rising warmth passing through him like the dawn rising over the mountains and warming the wet grass and leaves. It was a fever of happiness so intense he did not know whether to embrace it or spurn it as something dangerous. He remembered standing several years before on the other side of the world, on the slope of a different mountain, where he had watched the sun set over the barren high desert as the orange light moved slowly across the pine-needled forest floor until it vanished. He was looking for something then just as he was now, and once again he felt close to it, could almost reach it but the more he thought about it the harder it was to see. In the vast, heaving mass of the sea he saw a metaphor for the roving, free, and wild existence he wanted to live. He could stay on in Italy that summer and work for Dania's family as she promised, and he would never have to leave the beauty of that Italian warmth and he could work at what he loved and be loved at the same time. He began to feel restless in his happiness and so he stood and took a last glance at that ocean.

After walking around the mountain he reached the old rock tower and found Dania and Mike sitting together laughing by the large oak door barred shut. Matt felt a pang of discontent strike him at the sight of them. There was a hole just above the door, so Matt pulled himself through the hole and set his feet down in a stuffy room full of discarded wood and rubble. Matt followed the stairs past many cluttered rooms. The tower was larger than he had expected. In one room he found a broken bookshelf with a few books remaining. He picked one up, by Shelley, and read, "towers, thought's crowned powers." He continued up the stairs onto the roof of the tower with its stones glowing white in the sun. He looked out across the long stretch of beach and then to the large lake and the distant hills to the east, and he felt a wincing pain at the thought that this great joy would soon pass. He knew he had to take this feeling as a brief vision and not as a way of life. As he sat down on a worn rock and studied the rain-washed rocks of the tower he knew he would not stay in Italy that summer.

DIOTIMA: A PROLOGUE

Corinth, Greece, 514 BC

She awoke to red satin curtains hanging down around a bed. They swayed with a slight breeze. Beyond the curtains she saw the large wooden beams of a ceiling high above, and the white plaster between them. With effort she raised herself onto her elbows and looked down at her body. She was wearing a fine dress of brilliant white cotton, with gold stitching running down the tresses. A jade necklace lay across her neck, with an emerald as the brooch. It was the dress of a noblewoman. She knew this, and yet she did not know how. Who was she? Her mind tried to reach back to remember, but there was only a faint mist and a feeling that began to rise from the depths, growing until suddenly spasms shook her body and tears poured down her face. She screamed with the agony of loss. But it was more. There was love as well, love that opened the rift even more until it all threatened to subsume her. She could not look there any more. Her eyes opened and desperately looked around the room for something to save her, and slowly the feelings sunk into the mist, into the pandora's box from which they'd escaped, leaving her with only one image.

It was a young man that she saw, his first beard barely a light stubble on his face. He was handsome. Had she loved him? She did not know. She did not even know her own name.

She heard a doorway open and people running into the room. The satin curtains at the foot of the bed parted, and bright light obscured the figures standing there. She raised her hand to shield her eyes from the light, and began to see the robes. The satin on the sides of the bed parted as well, and there were more robes, and now she saw the faces of those who wore them. Old men with lowered heads surrounded her, unbelievably old, bent and weathered men who looked down at her silently. She looked at their eyes and saw that they were all closed. Blind, she wondered? Their robes were like those of priests, and yet she'd never seen the like. They wore simple white togas, but with a deep green border. There was something familiar about it, but nothing distinct. A large goblet was placed before her, and she took it eagerly, drinking deeply of water like none she had ever tasted. It seemed to transport her to a place of green leaves and flowing water, moss and pine needles, cool clean air. She opened her eyes, and the goblet was lifted from her hands. Silently the old priests turned and began to exit the room, their robes rustling on the stone floor. She yelled, "Wait! Please tell me why I'm here! Please wait!"

But they were gone and the door was shut. She tried to sit up, but it took enormous effort to lean her back against the wall. She rolled to the edge of the bed, and began to push one leg over the edge.

The door opened, and a voice called out, "I wouldn't do that just yet."

She pulled her leg back onto the bed and watched as a man dressed as the others entered the room. This one was different. He still had the look of youth, though he was older, gaunt and thin. His voice was deep and reverberated through the room.

"I know you have many questions, my lady, and I will do my best to answer them. As to your health: you've lain here for many months now, and I expect that it will require months for the strength to return to your body."

"Who am I? Why am I here?"

A look of surprise and awe crossed his face as he approached the side of the bed, and sat down upon a wooden stool.

"You do not know?"

"I can remember nothing. Only... a sadness that I fear to

152

acknowledge. And a face that I must have loved, for I remember something of love, but now it is mixed with that sadness."

"Curious." He paused, seeming to think deeply about what she had said. Still there was that look of awe, and it made her angry.

"Tell me what has happened!"

"Calmly, my dear. There is much that is new for me here too. Never has someone been given the light in the state that you were in."

"Speak plainly!"

I'm afraid the truth will sound ludicrous if you do not remember, although you are the proof of its truth. But I will not torture you with riddles. I'll tell it plainly. You... are... REBORN!"

He spoke the words with a dramatic lenity, each word emphasized as his eyes grew wide and bright, no word emphasized more than that of "reborn!"

She was silent for a time, the word swirling through her mind. It made no sense, and yet it was strangely compelling. She felt reborn, as if her body had passed into death and returned, but how? What did it mean? Reborn from what, from whom? At last she asked simply, "Who am I? What is my name?"

His eyes darted from hers to the window, and dwelled there for a time, strange unknown emotions moving across his face, the look of awe vanishing.

"The priests who brought you here did not tell me your name before they departed on their missions. I know nothing of who you were, only of who you are now."

"And who am I now?"

The excitement returned to his face, the exuberance of a child.

"You are Diotima, the wisest and most beautiful courtesan that Greece has ever known. You will live as a Queen in an age that despises women and cages them away in kitchens and courtyards while the men play. You will choose your own fate. Nothing will be forced upon you, and all shall be given to you. But now I must go. Think upon the gathering of your strength and we will meet again soon."

He rose slowly from the stool and walked toward the door.

"Wait, I have more questions! Please!"

"There will be time, my dear. For you there will always be...time."

"But who are you? Who are these priests?"

He paused at the door, not bothering to turn around.

"We are the children of the children of People. And we are the bearers of the Old Light."

The door closed, and she lay there in the silent room as the sun shone brightly in and the red satin swirled around her in the soft breeze.

A CAMP ON THE LAKE

The fields of furrowed earth, dry and bare, stretched to the pecan trees and beyond that, only sky. They drove on through the dry afternoon of November. Matt Baker looked over at his mother driving, and at his sister in the back seat. A sleepy silence reigned in the car and gradually the sky fell to the blazing orange of a southern sunset and finally to the purple glow of twilight. It was dark when the headlights fell across the stained dark wood of the cabin on the lake. The air was still and the cicadas silent. They stepped across the crunching gravel and into the stale air of the cabin. The circular couches and the dark table were still there. An old map of the Mississippi and a gaudy nighttime painting of New Orleans hung on the wall. He remembered three months earlier when his family had sat in this room watching the white vortex move across the television screen as if drawn to the watery eye of Lake Ponchartrain, one eye seeking another eye. And he remembered the strange calm and the forced humor that filled the room despite the endless news-talk: bearing down, predictions, dire, disaster, catastrophic. Three months ago. He walked to the cabinet and found a bottle of Jameson's.

"There's still some Jameson's left," he said.

"Make us some drinks, Matthew," his mother said.

He filled two glasses with Jameson's and ice. For his sister he added a lot of water to the third glass. He sat down and looked towards his mother as she lit a cigarette and the smoke shown opaque against her dark hair.

"It is good to get out of New Orleans. It's so depressing. I don't know if it will ever be the same," she said.

"It's quiet here," Matt said. "It reminds me of when we lived in the country on Nelson road."

He thought of the small house on ten acres of property and then he remembered the summer his mother spent recovering from her hysterectomy. In the afternoons he watered the flowers for her and in the house she played Chris Isaac and the music drifted out over the afternoon. He used to think about love and wondered if he would be a solitary man someday. Sometimes he rowed her around the pond in a boat. She seemed to like that. That was not long before the divorce.

Matt stood up and made himself another drink.

"Remember that fort Dad made me? It was just a frame of two-by-fours with clear plastic around it. You could see inside it. He missed the whole point of building a fort, of having a dark secret place to hide in."

His mother and sister laughed. His mother said, "he was always talking about all the things we were going to do, always coming up with ideas and I would get all excited about it. But then nothing ever happened. And then he was always hard on Matt about not having initiative to help him out around the property. I had to remind him over and over that he was not the best example of initiative for a boy to follow. Remember he would get on a kick and start pulling up all the weeds on the property only to have them grow back in a couple of weeks."

"Yeah, he'd get all concerned about the weeds or the grass but he left that ugly-ass shack standing for years, full of black widows, and he never put up a decent fence. We always had those old twisted fire-scarred fence posts with a few shreds of rusted barb-wire hanging from them."

They all laughed and then were silent for awhile as they remembered. And then his mother said,

"Matt, do you wish your Dad and I hadn't divorced?"

He thought briefly over all the years since.

"I don't know. It's so hard to imagine otherwise. I don't know if I'd be willing to trade all the experiences I had just to remove the painfulness of the divorce. Even Olsen had something to offer."

"He was the absolute opposite of your father. He was ambitious and he worked hard."

"I think what I really liked about Olsen was his energy. It could be annoying of course, like when he'd wake us up early on the weekends and we had to go out in that beat-up old pickup truck to gather monstrous rocks to build walls. Jesus, we made that place into a fortress with all the walls we built. And then he could be exciting too. Remember when it was winter and he jumped into the river and floated down and his brother and all of us were running down the bank shouting at him to get out? And afterwards his brother was just shaking his head and saying how Olsen had always been like that."

"Are you glad you decided to move to New Orleans?" asked his mother.

"I think so. It wasn't easy. But I probably got more out of it than I lost."

He remembered the summer before he moved, when they came out to the cabin on the lake and he was trying to decide whether he wanted to leave his home in Oregon with his father to go to New Orleans, where his mother lived. He had stood on the pier looking out at the stormy sky and the air felt heavy and full of purpose. It seemed then like even the storm was an expression of his feelings, the outer image of the dilemma raging inside of him. And then the lightning struck on the far side of the lake, and the thunder boomed across the water and the skies opened for the rain to fall and it was then that he decided to come to New Orleans. And the girl was no small part in it either. He had met her that summer when he was visiting New Orleans. They had enjoyed a few weeks together, drinking in the bars at night when back home it had been a struggle just to get a case of beer to drink in a house. She was the first girl he ever slept with, and one night they went to the French Quarter and they were sitting on a balcony looking out over the milling hordes of intoxicated people, the whole scene like some beautiful continuous decadence stretching back to the days when pirates roamed the waterways and spent their stolen loot in long debauches in New Orleans, and the cafés were full of coffee-drinking conspiracy and plots to rescue Napoleon from exile. And then on the balcony she told him she was in love with him and she wanted him to come to New Orleans and he felt helpless to disagree.

"God it is strange the way time moves. Sometimes I wake up from a deep sleep and for a minute I can't remember if I'm still a kid waking up to the sounds of roosters and chirping swallows, or a teenager in New Orleans with the sounds of cars and the hot steamy city right outside my window. Suddenly I remember that I'm twenty-two and nearly out of college and it all seems like a dream. In my dreams at least it's all of a whole. People and places from my life kind of blend together but it all makes sense. I don't really know what to make of the real world."

"Wait till you get to be forty-three," his mother said.

He laughed and then after a while he stood and walked outside. The night was warm and the lights of the houses across the lake shimmered on the black water. He could hear the water lapping with low sounds on the shore. It all went by so fast. But then sometimes you could climb outside of it and think it over, if only for a moment. He looked up at the stars and felt that old mystery burn through him until his hair seemed to stand on end.

THE SERVANTS OF ONE MASTER

October 3rd, 1760.

Carlo Goldoni crossed the Rialto Bridge and continued along the Grand Canal. It was a fine autumn day and the streets and canals of Venice hummed with merchants and wandering buyers. As he walked many people bowed to Goldoni but he was in a foul mood and he shouldered his bulk hurriedly through the crowd. Goldoni loved Venice. It was a city where anything could happen, and though a small elite held the reins of governance there was simultaneously a freedom not seen elsewhere. For Goldoni, the Renaissance had not died in Venice as it had in the rest of Italy. It had changed, of course. The explorations of Marco Polo had given way to the amorous heroics of Casanova and the days of Venice's commercial glory were fading. Still it was a city of love, art and raucous debauchery with more brothels, opera-houses and theatres than any other European city.

It had been a rough rehearsal session at the San Luca Theatre that morning. The season opened in a few days yet the actors were still struggling to remember the lines he had written for them in his new play, *I Rusteghi*. For more than ten years he had worked steadily to reform the commedia dell'arte, had attempted to give form and reason to the wild and vulgar Italian comedic style. Still the actors clung stubbornly to the old ways, often improvising when they failed to remember their lines.

And the damn stage was too large, Goldoni thought, too lavish and large for the middle-class world he wanted to display. But he could not complain too much. At 53, Goldoni was more popular in Venice than ever. After returning from Rome last season his play, *The Lovers*, had been a resounding success. These days, his playwriting was a far cry from the feverish pace of his youth. Goldoni laughed to himself as he remembered that season of 1750 when he had promised the Venetian public that he would write sixteen plays that year. He had succeeded.

But though Goldoni's star burned brighter than ever, a dark cloud hovered over the Venetian theatre. A young upstart, Carlo Gozzi, had written several publications denouncing the uncultured language and social radicalism of Goldoni's plays. Gozzi even accused Goldoni of destroying the great commedia dell'arte. Goldoni had responded to Gozzi with his own publications, but now it was time to take greater action. At that moment Goldoni was on his way to visit Gozzi at Colombani's, a bookseller and publisher, to settle the argument for good.

Goldoni paused and looked out at the canal. A gondola passed by carrying a pretty courtesan advertising her beauty as flocks of men gathered along the canal hurling flowers and gifts at her. In one swift movement Goldoni was twenty-eight again, a struggling young playwright in Venice, the jewel of Italy. For his new play he had hoped to cast the beautiful "la Passalacqua," Elisabetta Moreri d'Affisio, an actress who danced and sang skillfully and could even fence which made her perfect for the "breeches" role. He had come to visit her one evening at her home. When he arrived she asked him to join her in a gondola ride. Something unexpected happened that night. Perhaps it was the combination of the gondola's cushioned seats, the music rising into the deep night, and the lovely woman at his side. He fell in love with her.

Then Goldoni remembered how he had found out about Elisabetta's real lover, Vitalba, a few days later. He had threatened to quit the play and leave Venice forever, but Elisabetta called him to her home and threatened to kill herself with a knife if he did not forgive her. He relented, but revenge came nonetheless when he cast

160

her and Vitalba in the parts of unfaithful wife and rakish seducer. The people of Venice had loved it, quickly recognizing its similarities to the already well-known scandal.

Goldoni watched the courtesan pass by and then hurried down a side street. Soon he stood in front of the Colombani bookshop. He entered and walked down a hallway to a door with the sign of Gozzi's Club, the "Big Balls Society," hanging above. Goldoni opened the door and stepped into a spacious room with marble floors and large windows that looked out on the canal which shone golden in the late afternoon light. At a table by the window the lanky Gozzi reclined with a book in hand and a bottle of wine on the table. He went on reading. Goldoni coughed.

"I don't need anything," Gozzi said without looking up.

"Signor Gozzi, I believe you are in need of something."

Gozzi looked up with his piercing eyes and broke into a coughing fit. Finally he managed to say:

"Dottore Goldoni, I didn't expect you."

"Of course you didn't. You prefer to channel your venom indirectly."

"Come now, Goldoni, no need for anger. Sit down and drink some wine with me."

Goldoni pulled up a chair at the opposite end of the table as Gozzi filled two glasses of wine, drained his own and then refilled it.

"Up to your usual tricks, I see."

"A wise man once told me, 'the wine is the happiness.' Now tell me, Dottore, to what do I owe the privilege of your visit?"

"I have come to tell you that I resent your criticism. I desire a resolution of some sort. This foolish bantering cannot continue."

"It would not have started in the first place if not for your reckless disregard for the commedia."

"You are ignorant of Moliere. You are ignorant of reason. You are ignorant in general."

"Come now," said Gozzi, "you know as well as I that the characters in the commedia are living testaments to the heritage of the great Roman comedies. By slavishly copying Moliere you are but choosing to imitate an imitation, while the embodiment of the ideals you champion live on in the commedia you have rejected. You would choose a plaster cast of a Roman emperor to the real thing."

"Rubbish. The characters of the commedia have languished through centuries of dark ignorance. The fine structure of the ancient comedy has weakened through those years like a blood line left to the dogs. Moliere applied the reason of the ancients to the comedic form and came closer to the real thing than the commedia ever could."

"You and your beloved Moliere. I hear also that you are in contact with Voltaire?"

"Yes, I am fortunate enough to communicate with that light in a dark age."

"I despise them both. They readily tear down what exists while providing no alternative."

Gozzi drained another glass of wine.

"You would leave things as they are, never striving to improve?"

"Mark me, Goldoni, all of this… skepticism, will end disastrously. Even now the French draw closer to anarchy."

"They draw closer to liberty."

"What exactly do you think you will accomplish with all this? Your servants speak and think with the wit of the aristocracy. Your women lack all of the fragility and modesty proper to their sex. And you make buffoons of the nobility. Where will all this lead? All you will accomplish is the disruption of the social order, the breakdown of the natural scheme of things as God intended."

"If you despise my plays so much, then why don't you write your own? We'll let the public choose between us."

"That is easy enough. Audiences flock to see your plays and those of Chiari. Their tastes have been lowered from the high plateau that once was our happy lot. I could give them drivel and they would lap it up. ut I am more humane than you, Goldoni. Instead of slop I will give them a play in the old style, a fantastical and imaginative romp with masks and zanni and glorious music. They will dance and sing and all will be entertained."

"It is settled then. The stage is prepared, and we will do battle. The public will crown the winner."

"Exactly."

Goldoni and Gozzi shook hands. Goldoni left the room and Gozzi sat back in his chair and drank another glass of wine. He looked out at the canal and the gondolas lazily gliding across the water. So the battle would begin. But what had drawn him to this place and this imminent war with Venice's leading playwright? His thoughts drifted back to his childhood. As the youngest son, he had not been given the classical education of his brothers but was tutored by incompetent priests more interested in the house maids than in the young boy's learning. So he had often gone to the nearby library of the Soranzo family and there, with the musty smell of scrolls and old books, he found poetry. He read Dante, Cavalcanti, Petrarch, and Ariosto. The young boy learned all the grace of the sweet, pure Tuscan language. Yes, I am right, thought Gozzi, for Goldoni has purged the commedia of its poetry. He has replaced it with inelegant, common diction. But all will be remedied, he thought, as he picked up a piece of paper and began working on an old tale about love, the tale of three oranges.

Meanwhile Goldoni stopped on the Rialto Bridge to enjoy the late afternoon. He listened to a pair of lovers arguing as their gondola passed under the bridge. I will have to use that, he thought as he caught a few phrases from their conversation. Then he remembered when he'd first felt the urge to write down the words of others. At fifteen his family sent him to Rimini to study philosophy, a dull town until one day he saw a commedia troupe performing. He had never seen actresses before, and they enchanted him. When he went backstage to offer his praises the women welcomed him warmly and before long he'd taken to the road with the troupe.

They taught him everything they knew and before long the young Goldoni was writing scenari for plays. He loved the playfulness of the commedia, its music and its archetypal characters that seemed as old as humanity itself. Out of respect for his family he returned to school and managed to obtain his degree, but he was bitten, fatally, by the urge to write. And then one day a friend gave him a copy of Moliere's *Tartouffe* and Goldoni marveled at the fine structure of the play, how it ran so effortlessly like a finely tuned machine. Every complication came at just the right moment, building inexorably to that grand climax when the truth of moderation was revealed. That day Goldoni vowed that he would elevate the theatre of his people to that same degree of artistry. He would take the unruly improvisation of the commedia and lend to it the grace and precision of the French Neoclassicists.

And perhaps, if things went against him, he could go to Paris. Already he had begun negotiations with the Theatre Italiens. Voltaire and Diderot desired to meet him in person. But first he had to get through this season. He had one good play already prepared, if only the actors could remember their lines. Goldoni turned back in the direction of the San Luca Theatre for evening rehearsal.

THE LADY OF LAKE BRUIN: A FABLE

In the days when cars were still a novelty and the world moved at a horse's pace, two families feuded over the claim to dominance in the parish of Tensas in northern Louisiana. The Arobins were former French aristocrats who had fled the French Revolution to take root in the fertile land of northeast Louisiana. They owned a large plantation on the west bank of Lake Bruin. The Johnson family held the eastern bank, old English wealth now well-established in America. For years these families had silently warred through the purchasing of land for miles along Lake Bruin and the Mississippi, until one night at a parish dance the dispute turned bloody, and brothers of either family were killed. Since then, no blood had been spilled, so long as either family kept to their own land.

The Johnsons had a young daughter named Laura, the pride of the family. She played violin and sang to the delight of all. The pride of the Arobins was their only son, Alcee, a young man of wandering temperament but well liked by all. These two had never met nor were they likely to ever do so. Such a meeting would unravel the tenuous peace the families maintained.

One night at the parish dance, with the music soaring around the campfire and the beer and whiskey flowing freely, young Laura slipped away from her mother's gaze to walk along Lake St. Joseph in the moonlight. She stood on the bank looking across the silver sheen of the water. She sighed. She was not allowed to talk to the local boys and her life's joy was limited to the music she played. Her parents hoped to marry her to a wealthy man from New Orleans when she came of age.

She heard a rustling and looked toward the trees where she could see the small, glowing ember of a cigarette.

"Who's there," she asked.

"Someone you should not speak to, though I truly wish it were otherwise," responded a masculine voice.

"I do not think I that I should be denied the pleasure of meeting anyone," she responded with a voice that conveyed more self-assurance than she really felt.

"Then let me introduce myself. I am Alcee Arobin, the son of the family you despise."

He stepped into the moonlight with a vague smile.

"It is not I who hate the Arobins. It is only my family."

"But are you not Laura Johnson? And if so how can you deny the animosity of your family yet still be one of them?"

"As easily as I can play a song on the violin when everyone else in my family cannot."

They sat together on the bank and talked until they heard the anxious voice of Laura's mother. As they separated, they agreed to meet again the following year at the dance.

And so for several years they met only in the moonlight of Lake St. Joseph. But with every year they grew older, until the easy friendship they shared became marked by their desires for a life apart from the ones they lived. Young Arobin desired most of all an adventure like the kind he read in Homer's poetry. Laura wanted only the chance to know in real life the grand embodiment of feeling she found in music. And so when she told Alcee that she was soon to be married to a portly man of wealth from New Orleans, he determined to rescue her and west, perhaps to San Francisco. They decided that at night, when the lake settled to a stony silence and everyone slept, they would meet and go together to a private island. The next night, Alcee rowed across the lake and found Laura hidden in the willows. Silently they rowed together to a sandbar island where they built a small fire and talked until the first hint of purple dawn appeared in the east. For many nights they met like this, plotting their escape and the life they would live together.

The night of their escape the harvest moon shone down on the

166

lake. Alcee rowed across and found Laura in the willows. They rowed across the lake toward the Mississippi with their hearts aflame in anticipation of their coming freedom. But then Laura softly spoke to Alcee:

"I cannot leave my violin. We must go back."

"But we can get you one later, I promise."

"But this violin was my grandfather's. It means everything to me."

And so they rowed back to the Johnson house in the bright moonlight. The bow of the boat settled into the mud and just as Laura stepped out torches burst from the barn with men yelling.

"Go Alcee, you must leave now."

He pushed off and rowed frantically as the men leveled their rifles and shot at the vague white figure. Laura's father had been riding back from the fields of harvest when he heard his daughter's voice dimly float across the lake. He had summoned his sons and the workmen and prepared the trap. But every shot missed or hissed into the water as Alcee paddled into the safety of darkness. But there was one man, old Hugh Mcready. He had been a sharpshooter during the civil war and many young union soldiers had fallen to his aim. Calmly he propped his gun on a chair and leveled his aim at the dim white shape on the lake. His rifle shot boomed across the water and Alcee fell into the water, dead.

The following night Laura took a canoe and disappeared onto the lake never to be seen again. Some say she still haunts Lake Bruin when the harvest moon shines above the black water. They say you can hear her violin late at night like a wind through an thick oak forest as she searches for her lost love, Alcee Arobin.

SONG LYRICS

A FIRE IN YOUR BLOOD (2014)

Winter's coming, the world will shudder
The gods are waking, and kings are shaking,
The walkers stalking the cold north watch
And who can match their strength?

Down far south, from the devil's mouth
Comes a hope that floats in the stormborn's mounts
It's a hope that spreads from the mouths
Of those oppressed by kings and priests

There's a fire in your blood
And no one can hold you in the mud
And no, we can never get enough
Because there's a fire in your blood

Who could dream that the world would seem
Such a magic thing in the hands of kings
Who can't conjure fire or know desire
But through the whip and chain?

Comes a daughter of ancient fire
Who knows the gods and wild men
Freeing slaves so they make their way
Across the northern sea

There's a fire in your blood
And no one can hold you in the mud
And no, we can never get enough
Of the fire in your blood

Omens speak of the one who'll meet the cold
And burn it down

There's a fire in your blood
And no one can hold you in the mud
And no, we can never get enough
Because there's a fire in your blood

ANALOG GIRL (2015)

She wasn't much to you at first
Just a girl to slake your thirst
With a smile that could let you forget
She had pictures on her walls
Of mountains and waterfalls
And a record player by her bed
One night you met a girl
Don't remember, it's a blur
And your analog girl found out
So you met her at the bayou
And her tears meant she loved you
She had you without a doubt

She was your analog girl
With her records and her curls
And slowly she was much more
Oh that analog girl
Put your head in a swirl
And now your heart is sore

And so the months became the years,
Y'all's cottage was so dear
Somewhere between piety and desire
But hearts do often wander
When hers did yours grew stronger
Growing to a wildfire
You dreamed of her your wife
The partner of your life
A mother if she should seek
But she asked you for a break
"Not now, if you can wait"

She'd a new boy within the week.

She was your analog girl
With her records and her curls
But slowly she was much more
Oh that analog girl
Put your head in a swirl
And now your heart is sore.

ARYA (2013)

"High in the mountains of Carpathia, in a crypt carved into the sheer rock of a cliff, there lived an ageless vampire seductress, grown lonesome with the centuries. And so one evening she descended into the neighboring village in search of her prey of choice, a girl named Arya."

i came down from the mountains
at the first sight of the moon
i went into the village
and walked from room to room, singing

Arya, Arya,
we can float this boat down the river styx

i found her sleeping softly
the moonlight on her lips
i lay down close beside her
and i gave her my cold kiss
i said

Arya, Arya,
we can float this boat down the river styx

and home we'll never see
friends we'll never meet
the light we'll leave behind
down the river without time

i stayed there with her body
'til she felt as cold as i
i woke her with a smile

173

and i pointed to the night

Arya, Arya,
we can float this boat down the river styx

BRASS BAND GIRL (2008)

We were talking 'til the sun rose all the night long
Searching for the reason that we belong
And you call out to me to walk up to the sea
Believing once again that we are free

She's my brass band girl
She's my brass band girl
She's the candle that won't let me
Burn out

Seeing as we hadn't found our ways in life
Bound up and drawn together by our strife
And you find yourself again calling to the sun
Longing for the reason you belong

She's my brass band girl
She's my brass band girl
She's the candle that won't let me
Burn out

Somewhere beyond this place there's a dream we had
We lost it in the throes of this time we've had
And we're taken by the reasons calling endlessly
To be more than we have seen

She's my brass band girl
She's my brass band girl
She's the candle that won't let me
Burn out

MARDI GRAS SONG (2008)

Prytania and Euterpe on Mardi Gras day
Sitting on the balcony enjoying the parade
People are passing, I'm kiss your neck
Holding you close to me and dreaming of sex

It's so sweet to be alive, to feel the way we do
It's so sweet to be alive with you

Laying on the couch and I'm stroking your legs
We just made love and I'm loving this day
I see you looking at the sunlit street
I say, "hey lady, what you thinking about?"

It's so sweet to be alive, to feel the way we do
It's so sweet to be alive with you

And I'm caught one more time, I need you here with me
And I'm caught one more time, this moment we can keep
And I'm caught one more time, I need you here with me
And I'm caught one more time, this moment we can keep
This moment we can keep
This moment we can keep...

Walking St. Charles with the Zulu Parade
Had to catch a coconut and give it away
We're drinking wine and singing our songs
Oh tell me please, how long can this go on?

It's so sweet to be alive, to feel the way we do
It's so sweet to be alive with you

NEW ORLEANS TALE (2009)

here where the mississippi
snakes past the crescent city
a story i will tell you
of love and fallen glory

she was a southern beauty
well-born and scorning duty
he was a rich landowner
well-learned and growing older

they were married on
august first, a month of thirst
she spilled wine on her
satin gown from london town

his name was almonaster
the city's fencing master
one day in early spring
she flung aside her ring

"i will love you although
my fate will make us wait.
he grows older and someday
he'll pass away."

when the landowner learned
of her betrayal
he took action but
knowing he would fail

beneath the dueling oaks

177

a crowd of somber folk
watched almonaster win
the rich man had met his end

almonaster was tried
and found guilty
from the gallows he swung until
he was still

in her sorrow she leapt into
the river
now their bodies lie
in marble, side by side

THE BALLAD OF CODY BYRNE

OH, SEE THE SNOW (2013)

When we were strong and nothing called to us,
Eyes on our lives and now they are straying far
Why are they straying now that the snow begins to leave?

Please, don't you forget what it means
What it means, what it means,
What it means.

Hey, how'd it go? When did you end up there?
Warm and far from snow watching the sun go down,
Watching the olives caught in the fire of his song.

Please, don't you forget what it means
What it means, what it means,
What it means.

Sea catches you, carries you far from me.
There in a snare walking without my sight,
Talking away the hours and the days.

Please, don't you forget what it means
What it means, what it means,
What it means.

THE MUSE OF LONELY MEN (2007)

When your fire is flickering in the darkness of doubt
And your words are poor servants to the message you shout
And the daylight is far and the nighttime is near
And you want to give voice to your unspoken fear.
I will lend you an ear, I will call you my dear
I will take from your life your pain and your strife
And I'll call you the muse of lonely men.

When your voice is a croak in an echoless room
And your days run together like time in a tomb
And you're looking for more than what you have seen
But as you grow old it's a desolate scene.
I'll give to you song, I'll give to you wine.
We'll dance together, the evening will shine.
And I'll call you the muse of lonely men.

The beauty is broken the vision has fled
Your wisdom is rotten and soon will be shed.
The past is a mire that drained all your fire
After the fall of the elegant spire.
I'll be your bright future, your glimmering hope
In an age of confusion I'll be your rope
And I'll call you the muse of lonely men.

Your flowers are wilting in the heat of the sun.
You've lost every hand but you still think you've won.
You're betting that life won't take you away
But with every step you're nearer the grave.
Go raise up your hand and sing a last tune
With the evening on fire and the still, blazing moon
And I'll call you the muse of lonely men.

Yes, I'll call you the muse of lonely men.

THE NAZARENE (2016)

Gone today, the painted idle dreams that make you suffer
Crawl away, the perfect night and day that was your lover
And start anew, the search for a partner true

Washed away, the things you love they last but for a day
The sea sways, the trouble and the chaos always have their way
And so you bleed these songs, like a Nazarene on the cross

Til' you don't want to live a life that feels like always dying
These blackest thoughts the cost of always trying
For a life that cannot be sold

Hear her say, she wants you but she cannot come to love you
A child at play, your heart's a toy she fondles til she's through
And now you know the weight of a man whose heart is true

Til' you don't want to live a life that feels like always dying
These blackest thoughts the cost of always trying
For a life that cannot be sold

More than this, the hopes and dreams you've carried all your days
A dying wish, the portents and the stars already say
You'll hold this line as it strangles out your life

Til' you don't want to live a life that feels like always dying
These blackest thoughts the cost of always trying
For a life that cannot be sold

WINE DARK SEA (2015)

Sailing down the wine dark sea
Searching for memories
Of a time you were so divine.
What went wrong with our song
Blame it on a love so strong
Couldn't see right in front of me.

There's a cold hard edge to remembrance
The bitter self you see
Falling down in September's leaves
But you don't want
You don't want to believe.

Turn around if you're down
Head back to that little town
Take your place among the static race

There's a cold hard edge to remembrance
A bitter soul you see
Take these smiles and you run away
But you don't want to forget how to believe
To believe
To believe

There's a cold hard edge to remembrance
The bitter tree you fall
Take me back to September's leaves
But you don't know
Don't how to believe
But you don't know
Don't know how to believe.

MEDORA

What boy doesn't dream of the girl that makes the man?
In the labyrinth of desire who wouldn't take her hand?
Who knew what she would wake in you?
Who knew what you would meet?
The beast that lives in darkness,
The beast that feeds your breast.

Medora, Medora, I loved you like the sea.
Every inch of you surrounded me.
Every second I was clean.
When the doctors come to find you
Hanging in a dream.
Don't tell them that you knew me.
Just tell them it was me.

Our journey's waged, our ways began, spun upon a lyre
Ringing with the innocence of the children in the garden.
If I treated you a whore I only did it out of lust.
My love for you was primal. My love could never rust.

Medora, Medora, I loved you like the sea.
Every inch of you surrounded me.
Every second I was clean.
When the doctors come to find you
Hanging in a dream.
Don't tell them that you knew me.
Just tell them it was me.

When the story's done and over, and our lives have all been won,
Perhaps we'll walk along a river at the setting of the sun.

We'll talk about the old days, adventures still to come.
Perhaps our hands will mingle, and tighten into one.

Let go, let go, let go... Let go.
Let go, let go, let go... Let go.
Let go, let go, let go... Let go.

Medora, Medora, I loved you like the sea.
Every inch of you surrounded me.
Every second I was clean.
When the doctors come to find you
Hanging in a dream.
Don't tell them that you knew me.
Just tell them it was me.

MARION

Marion, mother of mountains, daughter of the sea.
I loved you with impunity. I loved you with intent
To marry our desires with a seed of discontent,
To ripen in the summer moon.
To ripen all too soon.

I'll always be a shadow man, a tracing of the sun.
What's here and what is coming, I'm always undone.
My shadow dance will tempt your fate and conjure you awhile,
But the shadow man is always bound for the lonesome shadow tower.

Marion, mother of mountains, daughter of the sea.
I loved you with impunity. I loved you with intent
To marry our desires with a seed of discontent,
To ripen in the summer moon.
To ripen all too soon.

The shadow of Medora always lay across our ways.
I'm sorry she was better at making me obey.
When silence comes to test you and the paths you have outworn,
Remember our survival in the shadow of that storm.

Marion, mother of mountains, daughter of the sea.
I loved you with impunity. I loved you with intent
To marry our desires with a seed of discontent,
To ripen in the summer moon.
To ripen all too soon.

Break out the wine, break out the song, I love to watch you dance.
In the labyrinth of my memories you still feel so warm.

I'd say that I was sorry but we know how it went down.
The gift is in the blessing, and the curse is now withdrawn.

Marion, mother of mountains, daughter of the sea.
I loved you with impunity. I loved you with intent
To marry our desires with a seed of discontent,
To ripen in the summer moon.
To ripen all too soon.

ROBY

Roby showed me to the door: "here is where you enter."
I held my breath and turned away,
Not yet to seek the other.
The way seems clear and happy when you see it from above,
Not yet to face the darkness,
Not yet to question love.

In Faenza's fair city high in my lonesome tower
Not yet beset with shadows, I looked upon the flower
Of all that life can give and take but would not seize the hour.
I walked along the river-bend but did not swim the water.

To stand upon the threshold of absence and desire,
To look at what is wanted, yet not hold it to admire.
She came in me and I came in her but our bodies had no part,
That day we shared the waters in the sauna of all art.

Roby showed me to the door: "here is where you enter."
I held my breath and turned away,
Not yet to seek the other.
The way seems clear and happy when you see it from above,
Not yet to face the darkness,
Not yet to question love.

THE END OF SOMETHING

Feeling like the end of something,
Nothing's left, I did my best.
Couldn't win her gypsy soul yet
Still I find, she loves my mind.

Mama's got a fire burning hot.
Couldn't leave it if she loves or not,
So caught, the end of something.

Where did I think this would lead me?
Texas pines, and she's divine.
Still it seems just like that story,
Hemingway and Marjorie.

Mama's got a fire burning hot.
Couldn't leave it if she loved or not,
So caught, the end of something.

POEMS

ALL THINGS REJECTED (2016)

All things rejected become things elected.
The beauty I predispose,
The magic that is close,
Smiles that win and tinted windows.
The aggravation of collapse and distress
'Til the smiling widow pats you on the back
Or says, "shame on you," gotta be true,
The jungle calls though it's buried under concrete.
This language makes the gods smile.

HERMIT'S SONG (2007)

Let my own self be all I need,
And the variations thereof.
May I change with every season
And though the winter's cold
Strangles my heart,
Let every spring bring a
Stronger change,
Just as the ice that wears the
Cliffs makes them wilder
And more serene.
May I find love in the glimmerings
Of my mind
And the sound of the sea
And the song of the sea.

I have wandered and rambled
And thought long on it,

And cursed myself for things done
But mostly for things not done,
Those acts that nearly appeared
Yet died the quiet death
Of the man who prepares to speak
But stifles it out of fear.
The long and lonesome shore
Will be my home,
And the wild waves my love,
The sunsets my birth,
The sunrise my death.

I HAVE A CRAVING FOR SILENCE (2007)

I have a craving for silence, and sleep, and death,
No more to be tempered in the furnace of the world.
I have tried to love and it has worn my soul,
For I walked too long and looked too far
For what was best found within.
Why scrape and beg for love?
Why try to force love like winter into spring?
Trust in something greater which your deeper
Need has designed for you.
Fools, all of us, to burn and fight and cry
And kill for a mere idea.
I know not love. I know only
Love that is wished-for,
And contrived and ultimately wasted.
Those long and sleepless nights spent
Thinking over every girl of pretty face,
Half expecting love to set right
All the temerities of a troubled life.
But I am through with searching.

I'll go to my burrow and live contented.

I'll fashion despair into an idol
Of that which was denied.
For though my rambling is done
My longing never will be.

Pour liquor in my veins, turn me wild
That I may like a vampire
Go hungrily in search of life,
That I may run through forests
Like a wolf at midnight.

I wish I could take a hammer to my life
And fashion it into a gleaming shield of bronze
Painted with scenes of heroic greatness.

I SAT DOWN TO WRITE (2007)

I sat down to write because a fire burned in my brain
The mad month of May like a naked woman on a speeding horse
Had caught me in her gaze and my heart was so full of aimless longing
That I dreamt of death or apotheosis.
      I shouted to the sky: what? What is it that you want,
      Daemon of my love and desire
      That has made me fill but a finger or hand?
      To the vast endless sky I submitted myself,
      If only for the streaks of fire that
      Rushed through my brain as I tried to sleep.

Tunneling through these wild holes in the consciousness of earth.
I am no prophet yet I could have fooled you,

Said the sage to the young buck who stood by an airy glen
One summer morning.
Call me Merlin,
For I have thrust myself between the rocks and the sea
And have learned the sorrow of humanity.
I am the prophet of love and desire and I've come to rid the world
Of spiritual pestilence.
       Hover over me, spirits beyond the mean,
       Speak your sacred words through my humble hands
       That they may float forever in the mind of humanity.
I am a humble shepherd in a lonesome desert.
Yet once I wandered far beneath a midnight moon to an oasis
Where languished twelve lovely women in states of undress,
Their cool shining skin in the light of the moon.
Hold me, help me, aim the fire that fills my brain.

I can remember so much, all of the prophetic longing
Of an eight year old in a barren land made green and lively
With the force of dream and imagination.
I cannot live without that though I have tried.
And even if I never tried what's there to say?
Only that I never refused the calling of the higher ones
To lead myself and friends beyond this confused realm
Where the thoughts are your gods.

A SHADE OF WINTER, A GLINT OF SPRING
(2016)

A shade of winter,
A glint of spring,
All that's dying
And all that's born.
I struggle to trace the curves

Of this infatuation,
To identify the single
Strand of hair that from
Her head entrances me so,
A voice that in the darkness
Said, "oh, yeah?"
A heart that for a moment
Said yes.

And where do these trails lead?
To mountains or to sea?
I have loved the sea.
She was soft and pliable
But always mysterious and elusive.
Can I love these mountains
As hard and unyielding as they are?
And yet I always knew the mountains
Would come, like the wood knows
Its future as the fire devours it.

A BLANK PAGE (2013)

A blank page
A blanc page
A white page
Is absence
That asks for fullness.
It is a question
That is pointed like a gun
To ask:
What is in you?
And so you reach to
Draw out the richness of

Your inner world
Facing always that first
Moment of sheer anxiety
When your mind goes blank
And the curtain descends
On the show.
A multicolored page may be more useful,
More reflective of what is in you.

MARCH ARRIVES (2013)

March arrives with the bursting of tiny new leaves on all the live oaks. In the late afternoon when the sky is clear the combination of brilliant blue and bright green is invigorating and calming to the eye. There is something reassuring about this time of year. Spring has come again and a long season of warmth is ahead, that warmth in which life at the smallest level becomes hyperactive, reproducing with abandon, and on up the food chain the transmission of sun energy extends. The long warm season ahead. It is the victory of light over the cold and dark, and it is primevally reassuring. In the void of space where temperatures plummet no life can exist, save upon rare spheres of matter that happened to have orbited a nuclear furnace ball at just the right distance; close enough to excite electrons into higher states of activity, but without unduly destroying or degrading those atoms that comprise our being.

COLD AND WORN THROUGH THE FLESH (2013)

Cold and worn through the flesh
As the morning wakes me.

In evenings I rage against the sleep,
Confident to wake again
With the heat of my evening thoughts.
And then I wake and the world is new
And I'm an empty vessel again.

SILENT ACCURSED HAND OF FATE (2013)

Silent accursed hand of fate
Sweeping away
Tangents of desire,
Plantagenets of hope.
In dreams we see what might have been
With tethers unleashed
And freedom dim.
My calloused hands reach for a guitar.
My thirsty throat inclines to wine.

Embarking upon a journey,
The ship leaving Greece at dawn
To sail the Adriatic to Venice.
Paul with his leather hat.
Amara with her glasses.

I've sounded the waves of my being
Sitting curled up in a warm shower,
The warmth showing me my deepest thoughts;
Riding that warmth into the vastness of what lies beneath.

The words came easily and happily,
A steady undercurrent of song.
There is only to relax and close your eyes
And the current will run.

COURSING DOWN THE AVENUES (2013)

Coursing down the avenues and alleyways of my mind.
Bright bitter morning wakes me.
I stumble out of bed like a drunkard
Fumbling for the light and bumping into walls.
Some distant place far from here
Where there might be less pain.
An island, or a beach beneath cliffs
Vast green and rolling plains

I see her serpentine.
I see her spider-like,
This succubus of late.
Into my own daylight I run
To escape the lair that has entrapped me.

On such mornings as these
To lay out my plots and schemes.
Mortality stands close.
I feel the burden of time
And the sadness of love.
And yet it will all end
In dirt or ashes.

ACROSS THE STRETCH OF A LIFETIME (2013)

Across the stretch of a lifetime, see the river running through twists
and turns, fast and furious here, slow and meandering there. I have

lived many lives already, and this current life is but one. It is a life of struggle at the moment, holding on to a love that has grown difficult, holding on to a way of living that is untenable, because the source of it has withered. I am no longer the man living on St. Roch with a heart overgrown with sadness, aching only for the touch of the girl he lost. I am now this man, still trying to make his way in the world, and less encumbered by his history. And yet this man lives in the same house, sits in the same room that witnessed all his sorrows. And so there is something of that era of emotional volatility and self-preservation that clings to him. He must leave here, this house or even this city for a time, so that he may return and rediscover this city in a new light, less as the place that could save his wounded heart, more as the place that his striving heart can redeem.

WE HAD A PICNIC ON THE BAYOU (2013)

We had a picnic on the bayou yesterday afternoon. It was a sunny day with a slight chill in the air. We debated points, talked back and forth, and at last seemed to reach some resolution. We cuddled for awhile with the sun warming us. Back at my house in the kitchen, I approached her sitting in a chair and spread her legs. We kissed and I pulled down her shirt to lick her breasts. We went upstairs and made long passionate love, as good as ever. Warmth and tenderness returned after so long. Changes will be happening, but for the first time since Mardi Gras we were truly intimate and loving again. Learn from it. Time apart can be good and create longing. Remember not to grow complacent about gift giving, for now when it is least expected it may be most warmly received. If it works, keep doing it.

MY CHILDHOOD IN OREGON (2013)

My childhood in Oregon. How to reach into it and explore its riches? The time we cut down a tree to honor my Grandfather's passing, and made a little cross which we affixed to the stump. The way those plants grew thick and tall along the canal in the summer, and the bees were thick around its tiny flowers, and I would run past as fast as I could hearing the feverish buzzing, feeling half thrilled, half-terrified that they would sting me and yet they never did. The day that my father and I chopped and stacked wood all through the morning on a cold fall day, and in the early afternoon went inside and my father made me some soup and a sandwich for lunch. Young Indiana Jones was on TV and we watched it together. He liked the production values of the show. The smell of the wood-stoves burning on the cold evening wind. The many nights I sat in front of our blue wood stove with its gold embossed lettering, looking into the bright heart of the embers through the glass window of the door. Floating around the pond on my little raft watching the dragonflies land on the grass at the shore, and trying to sneak up silently on the frogs that leaped from the bank into the water when approached.

Remember the dull ache of the heart in my first love encounters. Amber wanted to hold hands and it made me nervous. I was afraid to kiss her and was not yet an adolescent, was still clinging to some time when girls were just the ones you thought a lot about. But later there was Courtney, and there was no strange feeling when we wrestled together or when we kissed the first and only time after drinking a lot of tequila. We were in the kitchen stumbling around and bumping into each other, laughing loudly, and suddenly we were kissing and all I could think about was how awesome I was in that moment, how I was like my hero Indiana Jones. I didn't know what to do with her, but we kissed with our tongues in each other's mouths and rolled around on each other on the floor. I heard her mother coming down the hall and swiftly rolled off of her. The next morning we went boating on the lake and she said she didn't remember what happened, but surely she did.

Cold winter afternoons after school, the sun setting early and the great purple sky overhead, the first stars coming to light while I stood on the battlements of my castle's keep preparing for the night's assaults. There were two large juniper trees clustered together in the middle of a pasture, an island in the middle of a sea of short grass where cows meandered lazily. We built a fort there.

There were many maps on the walls of my room, and pictures of the places I had seen and loved: lakes at sunset, waterfalls, rugged snow-capped mountains, the ocean. A bookshelf held an Encyclopedia Brittanica from the sixties and books about archaeology. Sometimes I would climb under my bed and sit up under the headboard which was hollow. Here I was hidden and free, and could scratch words and images into the soft wood.

At night I would turn on the classical radio station and imagine scenarios to suit the music. Sometimes I dreamed of battles. Sometimes I dreamed of the girls I had crushes on, imagining us on a ship in the Atlantic during a storm, fighting bad guys and swinging across the deck on ropes.

Many days during the summer my Dad would drop us off at my grandparents' house. They lived in a victorian-style house in the country with perfectly manicured lawns and a vast, natural backyard of sage and juniper trees stretching to the canal. I would run outside jumping off the back deck and running down the sloping hill to Grandpa's shed, turning there to pass through the fallow garden, stopping here or there to look at the nests of the ants that always built their colonies where the dirt was dry. They were the desert ants to me, small and completely red with pincers and stingers, their nests consisting of a couple small entrances surrounded by many tiny pebbles. You only had to stomp a few times close to the entrances and within minutes hundreds would come running out of the hole circling the nest.

I'd continue out of the garden area and into the sage, darting around the dry, fragrant bushes until I came to the grove of junipers. There, around a couple of large volcanic boulders was a huge pile of juniper needles. This was the nest of the spraying ants, quite different than their desert cousins. They were larger with red bodies and gray, striped thoraxes, and they built ostentatious piles several feet high using juniper needles. It was rare to find a nest unguarded. Usually they were swarming over it as thick as the needles themselves, and at the slightest sign of a threat they would start to stand and aim their thoraxes at the target, spraying formic acid that smelled like hot sauce and made your eyes sting. They had large pincers that could take a good bite out of you, but they lacked a stinger.

Of all the ants though, my favorites were the wood ants. These were rare and difficult to find, and it may have taken me until adolescence to discover them. They could only be found under wood that had been left rotting for some time. Turning over the wood unveiled a series of tunnels. They were always relatively few in number, but fascinating in appearance: wine-red abdomens and black heads and thoraxes. They also showed distinct caste, with very large soldiers, larger than any ant I have ever seen, equipped with pincers capable of leaving quite a mark. I would take some of these soldiers in a jar and pit them against other kinds of ants. The desert ants and the spraying ants always won through sheer numbers, but not without the wood ant soldiers taking many casualties. The wood ants were my favorite because they were hard to find, noble and beautiful.

Years later my grandparents would often reminisce about how often I played with the ant nests, forgetting how much it had annoyed them and how they would call out from the house, "Ryan, what are you doing? Oh, just leave them alone and come inside." In retrospect those ants were my only friends on those summer days in the country where there wasn't anyone else around to play with.

My grandparents would let me go to the juniper grove but no further, because after that the land sloped down and they could not see me from the house, and there was a canal as large as some rivers. It was rumored that my grandfather could not swim, even though he had served in the Merchant Marines, and I always assumed that was why we could not go to the canal unless it was dry, and then we'd go to play with the crawdads that would get trapped in the leftover pools of water.

GREECE, ALWAYS GREECE (2013)

Greece, always Greece. The color of the water in the harbor of Nea Hora in Xania as I sat on the balcony writing in my journal. And through it all there is her, the memory of slowly losing the woman I loved. Did I hold on out of blind foolishness, or was there some intention behind it, some desire to acquire that painful, but most importantly, powerful and life-changing experience? Even now, three years later, I can transport myself to that balcony and feel my awareness of her in the room, feel my desire for her skin and hair, feel that unassuaged aching for her love. An experience that changed me but still not enough for what I wanted it to accomplish, if it was intentional. I wanted to come out of it with a fire under my ass, as Sara likes to say, driving me to do all the things I had planned to do. I thought that losing her would force me to make things happen. I thought my enduring love for her and desire to win her back was the answer to all the challenges I'd faced. It was not the answer. Maybe it was shortsighted of me to think that someone as self-interested as I am could ever be properly motivated to win someone else. And now I am facing those challenges, and what is my motivation? To be free to be curious and experimental and creative, to do the things I love to do. Give me an empty and quiet room where I am alone and nobody can hear me, that is all I desire for my basic requirements. After that, love and fun, and a feeling of being part of something larger and doing my part for the world.

A LITTLE WINE ALWAYS MADE IT BETTER (2013)

A little wine always made it better on Corfu. It brought out the lightheartedness that had been missing for a long time. Once, when her father was visiting us, she was upset that I hadn't joined them that afternoon, instead choosing to work on music. Later that day we drove to the highest point on the island, and she was raging at me as we stood there at the summit. I was about to take a picture of her in all her royal enmity, hair mussed and mouth a firm, angry pout, when one of those looks passed between us that always seemed to disarm even the worst of conflicts. Her anger melted into a reluctant but genuine smile. She put her arm around me and I took a picture that seemed to capture the dynamic of that trip: her, exasperated and yet unwillingly charmed once again, me looking wild with my hair scattered about, displaying an almost diabolical grin.

WHEN LAUREN CAME TO LA ROCCHETTA (2013)

We went to meet her at the train station in Orte. She was at an Internet cafe a few blocks away, and together we all went to a cafe. She looked matronly, and talked in a world-weary way of New Orleans. The friendliness between us was not strong anymore, although we laughed a lot together attempting handstands and cartwheels in the grass. We took a train to Livorno, and when we could not find a cheap room we decided to stay out all night or just sleep in a park. Later, Amara blamed me for not having taken control of the situation. It was the beginning of a destructive trip. Remembering that night that we argued and she must have told Lauren all, because Lauren laid it all out in plain detail: I was driving Amara away, and would steadily destroy every last thread binding us unless there was some radical change. I walked out of the room and sat against a fence in the backyard crying, crying for all the hurt in me, crying for my torment and for the love that was fading away.

Those were days of heavy drinking, rich Sardinian wine in my water bottle. It is easy to see how it drove me from my wits, again and again.

We spent our last night in Sardinia in a hotel room in Golfo d'Arancia, arguing miserably about the brokenness of our love, about how Amara knew that she wanted this to end. We decided we would go to Greece, and fulfill the original goal of our journey. I don't remember if I had to persuade her to give in to that or not. We made love, in the shower, for the first time in months. Greece ended up being the fulfillment of our shared journey.

HE LIVED HIS LIFE (2013)

He lived his life as if he was the hero of a fantasy novel, and yet in doing so he acquired more advantages than might be expected. After he came back from that experience on the mountain, everything was changed. He had gone to Pine Mountain, a relatively bare cinder cone that looked out across the high desert east of Bend. He brought with him a single jug of water, no food, and spent three nights there. An animal appeared to him on the third day, another one in the evening, and in the morning he drove home.

From then on, he believed himself capable of accessing a mystical energy. It would be tempting to say that he was delusional, and yet we must ask ourselves: if an idea otherwise irrational nonetheless serves to shape reality in a desirable way, is it truly delusional?

All of this worked well enough until one day the luck seemed to leave him. It was during a football game. He had been anxious before the game, uncertain of something, and then it happened. It was a freak accident, his own player running into him and falling on his knee, tearing his medial collateral ligament. For the next six weeks he was confined to a cast, hobbling around the school like a mere shadow of the man he had been. He believed it was his own fault, for losing sight of the sacred energy. He called it his fateful night.

After that day, he never again lived with the same conviction about his access to the energy from the mountain, although he felt it come and go at different times. In college, he tended to become intellectual and objective in his understanding of the world. After, a new energy came to dominate his life, that of love.

She sat on Royal Street, typing in the rain. It was one of those summer afternoon storms, rolling in swiftly and leaving just as quickly, bringing with it a welcome break from the heat, a cool breeze.

We are a generation so thoroughly drenched in the fictional representations of all eras that we have acquired a habit of living in many ages simultaneously. We are the unemployed of the great depression. We are the debauchees of the roaring twenties. We are the beatniks of the fifties and we are the festival hippies of the sixties. We are Whitman's humanity, and Poe's gothic sensibility, and Twain's spry humor.

He dreamed of summer rainstorms, of the balmy gray afternoons and the scent of grass and leaves in the air. He dreamed of her body naked in a bad, her brown skin under his hand. He dreamed of writing a story of all that had ever moved him, of writing it through

206

the course of the welcome summer. He could see the coffee table in the living room, its faux faded white paint. That table stood clearly in his mind as he imagined all this, a symbol of something. A table that looked older, looked quaint. A table that was solid and held things well. A stable, level surface. He wanted stability, and something he could build on.

PAULINA CREEK (2013)

Paulina Creek. Water flowing past grassy banks in the warmth of an August afternoon, the haze of light over the stream. He is tall and thin, brown-haired with bright, curious brown eyes.

See them wrestling playfully in the pool beneath the waterfall. He can feel himself hard against her down there. He wants to keep pushing against her.

At the camp and his father is building a fire. His father's girlfriend is making food at the picnic table, her frizzy blond hair surrounding her tanned face. "Should I make us some margaritas?" she asks in their couples voice.

Give in to sleep. Let the heavy warm wave wash over you, spinning you in the swirling darkness. Lean against the tide wall and let the sun warm you to the bone. Go back to the morning showers of adolescence, dreaming of this prison where you were free to spend all your time imagining. Is it a desire to return to the womb? To escape public scrutiny? A desire for death? Or a desire for the intensity of imagination?

Walking through alleyways of Sinarades by night, the cobblestones beneath your feet. She walks ahead of you, carrying your hopes and dreams, a small, adorable girl whose decision will break you in a few months. And yet you kept walking after her down those streets.

The tidal urges of desire. Yesterday I saw a crow swoop down and take a bluejay in its beak. Several other bluejays attempted to attack it, but the crow flew up and into the tree with the bluejay firmly grasped. One of the bluejays, perhaps the mother or lover of the prey, followed the crow and flew around it long after it was too late, singing a steady song of distress while the crows cawed their warnings in return.

When all is said and done, what is there to take away from it? I loved, miserably, deeply, and with an intensity that is both painful and joyful to remember, but most of all powerful. And now I feel far from it, in an era of love again, and commitment, and insecurity and ambition. Is it a dance that we must do over and over again, 'til the dance is over? Are we slaves to this impulse, to this tidal urge, building our worlds and tearing them down, again and again?

To close one's eyes and ride the current of submerged consciousness, carrying you to the farm where you grew up, playing with cities of mud on a summer day. Leaping swiftly from there to a park in Washington DC where you went as a nineteen year old to try and play again, by a small creek. You tried to build cities out of mud and instead you began to build a dam, because that was what you felt in yourself. A dam that held back that which is in you and is yours alone, that secret joy that must flow into the world.

When will the stories flow? It is good, perhaps, to close one's eyes and not try so hard to write. Attention is too focused and does not allow the finer subtleties to emerge. Writing itself is a distracting, attention-consuming physical act. I see her by the creek. Courtney in her sports bra and panties, wading into the pool. I have already jumped in and watch her with excitement. She sees me there, the silly, adventurous boy who is becoming a man. The boy who she used to tease mercilessly and yet he has become her friend. If I could be there to witness it I would look to the skies and laugh with a heart so full it could not be contained. I would look to the skies and see the work of the gods in action, the beauty of life actualized.

Let me find my way back to Oregon, to my childhood and adolescence. Let me find the poetry of it again.

THESE ARE THE DAYS (2013)

Living in this neighborhood. These are the days in which I wake in Sara's bed surrounded by walls of lilac, the bright sun streaming straight down from above. These are the days of early summer. In the evenings we open all the windows, and a good breeze moves through the house while the primeval murmur of crickets and bullfrogs rages in the night outside.

These are the days of wearing tan shorts without boxers, of driving through the French Quarter past St. Louis Cathedral and cursing the mule drivers who slow traffic, of passing through the CBD and coming out by the Convention Center to the fields around the old Mill with its twin smokestacks standing against a wall of thick, puffed up clouds, of driving down Tchoupitoulas to uptown houses and working a construction job that I hardly believe myself to still be doing, an almost comical disconnect from my professional and artistic ambitions.

These are the days of having Sara often scantily clad beside me, and of nuzzling her and kissing her all over and massaging her, of waking my lust again and again only to sense that she is not aroused, and so stifling the ache in me through distraction. I don't know what to do about it, and perhaps it doesn't matter enough to me to do anything about it.

I MET MARIKE AT MIMI'S (2013)

I met Marike at Mimi's one evening in April after having gone to a party on Gallier Street where Amara had briefly shown up. At the party I danced wildly after she left and then encouraged everyone to continue it at Mimi's. Arriving there the vibe felt different and I stood awhile by myself watching the dancers move to DJ Soul Sister's groove. I grew tired and began walking to the stairs when a man said to me, "this girl wants to dance with you." She was tall and beautiful, with dark hair and olive skin, and warm cocoa eyes that smiled. We began to dance, and the dance led to kissing, and the kissing led to a scooter ride back to my house. We made love that night and in the morning, and then I drove her to her hotel in the Quarter. We made plans to see each other that night at Saturn Bar. She met me there, but that night I decided to take someone else home with me.

THE SLOW PARADE (2013)

Will it be any different in a few months? The spectre of the present always outflanks the careful machinations of the future. We imagine a world that is perfect but we face a reality that has its own mind. A year from now the challenge will still be the same and will feel exactly like this. I am full, and I am tired, and I just want to watch *The Borgias* until I am sleepy.

How to circumvent such whirlpools of bodily desuetude? I remember the temple of Poseidon at Sounio. What did I ask him? I asked for her, but I also asked that if greatness meant losing her then let me lose her. It was not a turning point. Still it is amazing that we continued as long as we did after that, and how often I spurned our connection vocally by saying things like, "I realized that I'm not in love with you anymore, and that it has faded." Such a fool, and yet foolishness often serves a purpose. I wanted out of the misery of loving her, of fearing for her loss. I wanted a way to become greater, and I found it. Through sorrow and desperation I came to know a larger self, ironically more confident and less fearful than the man she loved. And now, years later, what have I become? A man with great strength, and yet still testing his abilities, still slightly unsure about using his abilities, about their ascendancy. And yet he continues to realize the largeness of his soul, that soul kept hidden for so many years, and still a little shy and distracted. It is all here though. All that is waiting and expecting, the child that grows silently, is here in this subtropical farcical world I have chosen as my home.

Ilias the Greek, wearing his red shirt and getting drunk at his own bar with his two American friends. He took a knife from under the bar and gestured how he would cut the throats of the politicians who were destroying his country. He said, "who will be there to carry it on?" He never explained what he meant. He said, "I am fifty-seven years old and I am going crazy," and I believed him. He cried in front of us, cried because of the stress of running a failing bar, cried for love lost and youth squandered and nothing to look forward to. We comforted him as best we could, drinking Tsikoudia, the distillate of already fermented grapes.

I have been to Greece and it was not what I expected, and yet I have remembered it every day since.

In Europe I began to drink wine from my water bottle, whenever I pleased, because so little was expected of us. The culture of intense focus and productivity was lost, and all that mattered was that you were present, which wine helped. Sure, the relationship was going to shit and it helped with that, but most of all it just helped me stay present and connect with those around me. I'd come from that college student mindset of always looking for the answers to questions in the books of others. I sought out information about everything, studied exhaustively while the world reeled on around me. I did not divest myself of my scholarly habits until I returned to New

211

Orleans, and had no choice any longer. The old palliatives failed me then. The mere words of another, even the most intelligent human on earth, could never be enough to quell the ache cutting me up. And so I drank, and I went out, and I became human again. I learned to connect and feel and decipher the symbols of the world with my own alphabet.

There were berries all around, bright green and shiny leaves that shimmered in the afternoon sunlight. There was dry earth underfoot and green sharp and pointed leaves. We picked berries all afternoon, glancing at each other sometimes and smiling, but saying little. When it was over and we had turned in our day's work and received our pay, we took the bus together back to the city. We were shy, having spent so many hours in our minds in the meditative peace of repetitive labor. Slowly we inched our way to a connection. We talked of commonplaces and then fell silent a while before resuming another commonplace. Luckily I remembered the bottle of wine mixed with water in my backpack. I offered it to her and she accepted, laughing at the thought of my quotidian water bottle hiding such a source of freedom from reality. When we arrived in the city I invited her to my house to listen to records. I had bought a turntable and a few of my favorite records. As the cool evening breeze blew through the window and Joni sang in minstrel melodies we shared a bottle of wine and made love on the rug the Honduran man next door had given me a week before.

I remember going to see my Czech-New Orleanian writer Andrei Codrescu at the Gold Mine Saloon that lonely autumn of the September that never ended.

I am twenty-nine and yet there is a soul as young as rain in me. Sometimes I start to feel myself aging, for the first time really, in the way that men begin to feel a little slower in the mind, a little less flexible in opinion, a little less virile physically. And yet there is something that has been growing and gathering strength for a long time, a poignancy and a relevancy that is just coming to fruition. It is so astounding that I scarcely acknowledge it sometimes, and yet I feel it around me, in glances and softly spoken words, a refractory feedback that speaks of something gained effortlessly and without conscious determination.

I stood on the bare, rocky summit of pine mountain and looked out across the desert of my homeland, and I saw armies kicking up dust, I saw a world that had lost touch with its home. I imagined coming down from a mountain, Zarathustra is now all I can picture, and carrying forth a new vision for humanity. I imagined a tribe of people living on Elk Lake, searching for a different way of existing that was closer to our roots. I saw all this before I knew of the Paleolithic diet, before I knew of organic as a farming concept, before I knew the way the world would start to run. It has all started to happen now. What else came to me in those first visions? Love, as a guiding force, as the only emotion to be sought out above all others, the lighthouse shining in the midst of the raging storm.

What a waif of a town I can claim to come from. Those nights come to mind of stealing wine or tequila from our parents and wandering through the subdivision under the undiminished Central Oregon stars. And yet we always sought out the natural places, such as the lava rock hill where it would be too much work to raze down for house-building. It was like a fortress, and we went there to sit beneath the stars and drink our stolen liquor. What was life to me then? As grand as it is now, as fulsome and majestic, and yet I only lacked details. The time Courtney and I snuck into the sewer treatment facility and drove golf carts around crashing into each other until someone spotted us. Such small, rural adventures, and seeming so far now, and yet the spirit is always the same. There is a glint in the eye, a lightness in the heart that never leaves us so long as we remain here and open to the world. To be human is to laugh with the glimmer of starlight, for there is something to this world that forever escapes understanding and yet trembles in our molecules.

AND IF I WANT TO BE GREATER (2013)

And if I want to be greater than Goethe
I must know the ache of the flower
Driving its way into sunlight,
Must know the tribulations
Of the snail on the log,
The cockroach in the sink,
The lizard on the leaf.

CREDO UT INTELLIGAM (2005)

The writer writes to fight the sleep
That in his soul would dwell,
The dreamless sleep, the darkness deep
That makes his life a hell,
For in the Word and cunning phrase
A crackling light or flame
To melt the ice and stiff malaise
That otherwise would maim.
The writer and his darkness deep
As stark as night and day,
But each to each, to laugh or weep,
In marriage bound to stay.
He cuts the rope that round his throat
Would surely end his life
With words like gleaming steel, precise
And forged to icy point.

The knee-deep winter mire,
The death to hopeful fire,
Is waged in holy warfare

With the summer's sweet attire.

The battle's waged, the mind will flame,
And poetry's the daughter.
The battle done, the sun will set
But on will live the fire.
As grapes compressed and left to rest
Will gain a joyful flavor,
So time's delay and sunshine's crest
Will leave the wine to savor.

THE END

ABOUT THE AUTHOR

Ryan Gregory Floyd is a writer of songs and stories and 2017 marks the dual release of a new compilation CD, "A Fire In Your Blood," and the publication of his first collection of fiction, *The Ballad Of Cody Byrne: And Other Stories*, both backed by an extensive US tour through late 2017.

"A Fire In Your Blood" is an exclusively direct from artist-to-fan compilation CD of Ryan's best originals and cover songs. The album kicks off with Ryan's dark but alluring pop ode to Daenerys Targaryen, "A Fire In Your Blood," and follows up with a stirring live rendition of Kris Kristofferson's, "Sunday Morning, Coming Down." "Arya," a Balkan influenced gothic fantasy of vampiric seduction, "Stable Song," and "Ghosts" round out the next few tracks. The album is a testament to Ryan's ability to channel diverse genres into a captivating and compelling live show.

The Ballad of Cody Byrne is a fiction collection containing two novellas, ten short stories, poetry, and lyrics dedicated to author and poet Jim Harrison and singer-songwriter Leonard Cohen, both of whom passed in 2016.

Ryan's professional career in music began in 2014 with an 18-month focus on writing and recording that yielded two LPs (Of Muses and Men, Hekatombaion), three EPs (Sara, Equinox, The Red And The Black), and a live LP (Live At The Hi-Ho Lounge). The next 18 months saw a focus on live performances, both solo and with multiple bands, resulting in over 200 live shows and a new live EP (The Nazarene) in 2016. The publication of *The Ballad Of Cody Byrne: And Other Stories* marks the official start of Ryan's entry into writing as a professional career.

When not on the road, Ryan divides his time between his hometowns of New Orleans, Louisiana and Bend, Oregon.

For more info, please visit http://www.ryangregoryfloyd.com/.

www.ingramcontent.com/pod-product-compliance
Lightning Source LLC
Chambersburg PA
CBHW020113180626
46812CB00006B/2578